What the critics are saying…

"*Heat level: O(rgasmic): Young Vampires in Love* is an utterly delightful vampire paranormal erotic... very original... The adventures of Lynette and Darlene, who have lived in seclusion for over 30 years, provide for quite an amusing ride... The erotic scenes in this book are **PIPING** hot. There are a couple of scenes in a club that literally had me squirming on my seat. ...this book certainly is one to try." ~ *Just Erotic Romance Reviews*

"Mardi Ballou is an exceptional author who has taken vampires to a whole new level. They show a level of humanity not normally seen in stories about vampires. Vampires can love, and be hurt by love, just as humans can. I found this story very intriguing and I can't wait to see what she has in store for us next." ~ *Fallen Angel Reviews*

"...funny and entertaining... This interesting novel excellently combines well described characters and humor with really hot sex, romance and BDSM... a refreshing and unusual insight into the love lives of vampires, this story is definitely a must-read!" ~ *Mon Boudoir*

"…filled with lots of searing, scorching sex, just about any kind you can dream up. Certainly, Mardi Ballou does not lack in the imagination department! Better have a cold drink nearby when you read this one. *Young Vampires in Love* is guaranteed to make anyone's blood boil!" ~ *The Road to Romance*

Young Vampires in Love

Mardi Ballou

YOUNG VAMPIRES IN LOVE
An Ellora's Cave Publication, April 2005

Ellora's Cave Publishing, Inc.
1337 Commerce Drive, Suite #13
Stow, Ohio 44224

ISBN #1419951831

Edited by: *Heather Osborn*
Cover art by: *Syneca*

Warning:

The following material contains graphic sexual content meant for mature readers. *Young Vampires in Love* has been rated *E-rotic* by a minimum of three independent reviewers.

Ellora's Cave Publishing offers three levels of Romantica™ reading entertainment: S (S-ensuous), E (E-rotic), and X (X-treme).

S-*ensuous* love scenes are explicit and leave nothing to the imagination.

E-*rotic* love scenes are explicit, leave nothing to the imagination, and are high in volume per the overall word count. In addition, some E-rated titles might contain fantasy material that some readers find objectionable, such as bondage, submission, same sex encounters, forced seductions, etc. E-rated titles are the most graphic titles we carry; it is common, for instance, for an author to use words such as "fucking", "cock", "pussy", etc., within their work of literature.

X-*treme* titles differ from E-rated titles only in plot premise and storyline execution. Unlike E-rated titles, stories designated with the letter X tend to contain controversial subject matter not for the faint of heart.

Also by Mardi Ballou:

Pantasia III: Forever on the Isle of Never
Fangs 'n' Foxes in the Nibbles 'n' Bits anthology
Pantasia II: For Pete's Sake
Pantasia I: Hook, Wine and Tinker
Photo Finish

Young Vampires in Love

Chapter One

From Veronica Vampira's Secret Diaries:
Philippe had been the prince of my soul. One dark and storm-
tossed night, I saw him put his arms around Gwendolyn, the vile
vixen who led men to their doom and destruction. Though my
head chided me to abandon my foolish fancies and forget fickle
Philippe, my hard-pressed heart began to beat rapidly, pumping,
ever pumping forth my intense agony, and I fell into the deepest,
blackest of swoons…

A fine mist swirled across an early spring night sky, descending near the decrepit remains of an old house. Once known as the Dupont-Monroe Mansion, the structure lurked on a now obscure cul-de-sac in San Francisco's Pacific Heights, overlooking the gleaming Golden Gate Bridge.

The mist slowly became solid, taking on the features of an elegantly dressed man. Once on terra firma, he brushed himself off, then, curling his lips in disdain, surveyed his surroundings.

Laurence de Cormignac, the Comte du Montnoir, sighed and prepared to enter the home of Lynette Loring and Darlene DeMars. He shook his head in regret over the fiasco that forced him to make this journey. Several decades before, ignoring his better judgment and the wisdom of centuries, he'd transformed Lynette and Darlene. He gritted his teeth, reminding himself how he'd succumbed to their fresh-faced American charm. Now he was paying the price for his lapse in giving these two unworthies the gift of immortal life. He'd rarely ever made errors—and never before or since had he made such potentially costly ones. But gloomy, negative thoughts were of no help now.

Flickering candlelight from inside the mansion cast shadows on thick drapes closed against the beckoning light of the nearly full moon. The Comte had just lifted his hand to knock on the door when the sound of raised voices alerted his supersensitive hearing and gave him pause. He quickly identified each speaker.

Lynette, who had the lower voice of the two, said, "It's all your fault that our manuscript was rejected. You keep insisting on writing sappy-sweet love stories—and that's what's killing our sales and threatening our careers."

Darlene choked out her response, her voice rising to an unattractive squeak. "I refuse to compromise, to make our heroes and heroines succumb to your—" *gasp, gasp,* "—cynicism. We don't have to follow them into the bedroom... Our primary, Veronica Vampira, has her fans who adore her just the way she is. We don't want to alienate them."

"Do you seriously think her fans want Veronica to shrivel up from terminal horniness—not to mention boredom?"

"Not everything's about sex..."

"Oh yeah? So how come, after three successful books and two admittedly less successful ones—but still getting *some* sales, our latest manuscript was bounced back to us? Things have changed since we started writing. Readers want more now."

From bad to worse, the Comte thought. So now even their dubious success in publishing trashy novels for the hoi polloi was on shaky ground. The two women continued to bark at each other, their exchanges becoming more rapid, high-pitched, and irrational. The Comte had heard enough. Clearly they needed his guidance to avoid the disasters waiting to overtake them from every side. Like the cavalry in a western, he'd arrived not a moment too soon. He rapped on the door thrice. After getting no response, he knocked again — more forcefully.

* * * * *

"Are we expecting company?" Darlene stopped in mid-whimper to ask Lynette.

Lynette scowled. "Why should tonight be different from every other night? No one ever comes around anymore. I think the last time we had a visitor was 1999."

Darlene wrung her hands. "I don't want company. I hoped we could spend the next several hours working on this manuscript so we can send it back to our editor."

Lynette shrugged. "I think we should just bury this one and start over, but not tonight. For one thing, whoever's at the door doesn't sound like he's going to go away."

Darlene rose. "I'll get rid of him."

It was out of character for Darlene to be so decisive and inhospitable. Lynette occasionally got flashes that her friend had undiscovered layers beneath her sweetness and light exterior. Feeling ornery, and curious as to how far Darlene's darker side went, she followed her and said, "Or you could invite him in. For a snack."

Darlene frowned. "Now none of that. We stopped feeding from humans years ago. Besides, we've already eaten…"

Lynette rolled her eyes. "Yeah. O positive *again*," she griped.

Darlene put her hands on her hips. "You know I had a coupon—and the blood bank's been running a sale…"

Lynette was about to make another comment about those damned coupons when Darlene opened the door—and the Comte du Montnoir swept in.

Oh shit. Their nominal master, the one who had transformed them both when they'd been students on vacation in the French countryside, was not in the habit of making house calls—especially on the least favored of his flock. Hell, he also had a well-known aversion to leaving French soil, and he particularly hated California. His presence *chez eux*, as he'd say, was probably not an announcement of good news. The scowl on the Comte's face—he looked as if he'd just spent an hour under the desert sun—confirmed Lynette's suspicions.

"Monsieur le Comte," Darlene said, addressing him by his preferred title. "To what do we owe the pleasure of your company?"

Cripes. Darlene was practically *curtsying* to him, Lynette thought in disgust. Lynette was just as intimidated as anyone by the Comte, but she'd be damned if she'd act as wimpy as Darlene.

The Comte shrugged off his magnificent black silk cape, revealing his expensive designer eveningwear. Probably Armani. He held the cape out. Darlene, clad tonight in her Carl's Comfort Coffins T-shirt and fraying sweatpants, rushed to take the elegant cape from him. "I am afraid it is far from a pleasure," he said in his deep, rich baritone, brandishing a thick creamy-white envelope in his hand.

Making a moue of distaste, he put the envelope down on their slightly dusty mahogany end table. "But first things first. I've come a long way and am in need of refreshment. What can you offer me?"

Lynette inwardly groaned. She wished she could snap her fingers and instantly stock their pantry with gourmet specialties.

"We have some lovely O positive," Darlene said softly.

The Comte shrugged his elegant shoulders. "And what else can you tempt me with?" Lynette winced at the sarcasm in his tone.

"Just the O positive," Darlene said even more softly. Lynette restrained herself from catching her friend's eye and mouthing, "I told you so." Anyway, Darlene was avoiding eye contact.

"O positive," he murmured, pursing his lips. "But of course that is what the two of you would have. The most ordinary variety. Very well, any port in a tempest and all that. Bring me a glassful."

The Comte went to their black leather couch and, moving so unobtrusively Lynette wasn't sure she'd seen him do it, brushed off the seat. Then he sat.

I hope she doesn't use a plastic tumbler, Lynette thought. Thankfully, Darlene remembered to use their good crystal, which now gleamed with the ruby liquid. Her fingers trembling, Darlene handed the drink to the Comte. He drained the glass in three large, but refined, swallows. He then handed it back to Darlene, who scurried off to the kitchen and returned quickly. When both women were seated in the chairs opposite the couch, he held the envelope out to them.

"Do you know what this is?" he asked, baring his teeth.

Lynette and Darlene looked at each other. In the Comte's case, they knew his bark was at least as bad as his bite. Lynette hoped she wouldn't say anything he'd regard as foolish, but she wanted to get the bad news over with. "It looks like an invitation of some sort."

"Bravo!" he said. "It is exactly that. An invitation—one no one wants to receive. And it has your names on it."

"What is it, Monsieur le Comte?" Darlene asked.

"I shall read it." He cleared his throat. "'Lynette Loring and Darlene DeMars are hereby invited to the Palais Royal de la Nuit in Paris for the Bicentennial Awards, le 14 novembre.'"

"But, with all due respect, what's wrong with that?" Lynette asked, speaking before she thought. "Darlene and I haven't been back to France since…well, since our transformation."

"I have not finished," he growled.

"I'm sorry," Darlene said.

"Do not apologize *yet*," he hissed, glaring at Darlene. "Not until you know *why* you should apologize."

Darlene sat back in her chair and looked down at her lap.

"Do you know about the Bicentennial Awards?" the Comte asked.

"Can't say I do," Lynette said, "but they sound impressive."

He narrowed his eyes and gave her a withering look. Lynette, determined not to let him cow her the way he did Darlene, suppressed a nervous squirm. "Many of them are. These are awards presented by the cream of international vampire society, the hundred leaders of our councils."

"Still sounds good," Lynette said, half to herself.

"There are some awards for creativity in the arts…"

"You mean like our books," Darlene piped up.

"Hardly," the Comte replied, actually shuddering. "As I was saying, awards for the arts, for leadership, for bravery."

"Sounds like we should be honored to be nominated," Lynette said.

"Though you are young, there is no excuse for such *naïveté*. Not every award is an honor. Now if you will both be quiet and listen, I shall read the rest."

Lynette bit back her response and did as the Comte said.

"'Lynette Loring and Darlene DeMars, from the Atelier Montnoir, have been nominated to share the award for *Most Dull and Boring Vampires*. Their presence at the ceremony to accept the award or congratulate the recipients would, of course, be most highly appreciated.'"

Lynette and Darlene groaned simultaneously and looked at each other.

"Is this a joke?" Lynette asked when she'd recovered her senses sufficiently to formulate a response.

The Comte threw up his hands. "*Mais non*, this is no joke. This is the most serious of events. Do you realize that if you win—and I hesitate to use that word in this situation—if you actually *win* this heinous award, you will have to drag around this title with you for the next *two* hundred years?"

"I know what bicentennial means," Lynette grumped.

The Comte snorted. "And, I must tell you, with you coming from the Atelier Montnoir, *my* personal lineage, I have much to lose here, too. If you come away with this dubious honor, I shall be a laughingstock amongst my peers. For the next two hundred years, I shall be the butt of jokes and derision, just like poor Guillaume Risible has been for the past two centuries. You would do this to me after all I have done for you?"

"No, no, dear Comte, of course not," Darlene said hurriedly. "But I don't understand. Why were *we* nominated for this award? After all, we just sit here, quietly, writing our books. We never bother anyone. Gosh, we order everything delivered—never even go anywhere anymore."

"*Exactement*," the Comte said, shaking his head. "You have just answered your own question."

"I have?" Darlene asked.

"Let's face it, being a coupon queen does not exactly make you…*exciting*," Lynette said.

Darlene pouted.

"It is not only the 'coupon' business," the Comte said. "*Sacre bleu*, both of you, *look* at yourselves. Just look at yourselves."

Of course, without the ability to see their reflections, that was no longer an easy option. But Lynette looked at Darlene, who was wearing her favorite red sweat suit tonight with the unfortunate T-shirt. Her slightly frayed and pilled sweat suit, with the loose elastic at the waist.

Darlene, the shorter of the two, had gotten a bit soft since they'd begun relying exclusively on the blood bank as their food source. Before that, their occasional hunts and the variety in their diets had kept them both in the same trim shape as their early days.

Darlene had been twenty-two when they'd undergone their transformation in 1972, Lynette twenty-three. Now, more than three decades later, Darlene still wore her brown hair long and straight in the seventies style, her blue eyes and pale lips free of cosmetics. Lynette knew that, these days or nights, she didn't rate much higher than her companion on the glamour scale. Her blue velour tracksuit thankfully bore no advertisements. While slightly less worn than Darlene's outfit, the jacket was being held together by several safety pins in lieu of the no longer functional zipper. Though she wore her black hair pulled back into a bun, Lynette had to admit this was also a haphazard, sloppy arrangement with hairs straggling loose. She usually put on lipstick and outlined her brown eyes with a brown pencil in a Cleopatra style, but she'd run out of her cosmetics some time before and not replenished the supply. Why bother?

The Comte, who always surrounded himself with the most elegant and chic women—and men—was looking at them with utter contempt. And then he buried his head in his hands. "It's hopeless," he said. "Hopeless. I shall be drummed out of my club, a source for derision everywhere I go, once you *win* the award. The name of Montnoir will be dragged through the mud. It's enough to make me look for one of those vampire hunters and…"

"Monsieur le Comte," Darlene said, "don't talk this way. Surely there must be something we can do…"

Lynette, who was thinking it might not be so bad sending the Comte's name and address to a vampire hunter, bit her lip in shame. Even though she had her issues with the Comte, she had to admit he had a point. Hadn't their latest manuscript come back tonight with a big fat Rejection stamped on it? After their first three vampire romances topped the bestseller charts, the next two books had done somewhat less well. And now their editor, Edna Edmore, had just described their work with the same words the awards committee used about them— dull and boring.

Lynette sighed. She hated to admit that maybe there was something to what these people were saying. The zing had gone out of her and Darlene's lives (or was that unlives or dislives? Oh well, this was no time for semantics.) Lynette realized they'd have to do something quickly—both to get out of the running for the dreaded award and to restart their stalled writing careers.

Darlene was actually wringing her hands. "Please, Monsieur le Comte, tell us what we should do so that we won't get this award."

The Comte exhaled heavily. "It may already be too late."

"You said *may*, Monsieur le Comte," Darlene said. "That means that maybe there's still a possibility for us to avoid this cruel fate."

He drummed his long fingers on the end table and appeared lost in thought. Lynette suspected the old goat was just extending the moment for dramatic effect. After all this time, she was starting to get wise to such tricks. Darlene, who never seemed able to find silences comfortable, started to speak again. Lynette shook her head, and—thank goodness—for once Darlene picked up the signal.

At last, the Comte began to speak again. "You are fortunate to be here in San Francisco. Fortunate, of course, is a relative term. You have the misfortune not to be in France. But as you chose not to make your home there, San Francisco is among the best of the other possibilities."

"Seeing as Lynette inherited this place before our transformation..." Darlene started.

The Comte held up his hand, and Darlene fell silent. Lynette knew he didn't appreciate having his long-winded spiels interrupted.

"As I was saying," the Comte continued, his voice now sounding a bit like a drone. "Here in San Francisco, you have many opportunities for an interesting, uh, *life*. There are clubs, shops, shows, a whole cosmopolitan panorama. There is no reason for you to follow a narrow existence here. You should expand your horizons beyond an O positive lifestyle."

Lynette shook her head. Though she'd never express herself the way the Comte did, she often said the same thing to Darlene. But she'd fallen into as deep a rut as her friend. Still, she wasn't about to admit any of that to the Comte right now. Even though she agreed with him.

Darlene, on the other hand, appeared instantly ready to fall in line with what he wanted. "Monsieur le Comte, there are so many places—far too many for us to sort out quickly. And, as you say, it is urgent for us to show the committee we do not qualify for their award."

"Yes."

"So perhaps you can recommend to us where we should begin. What should we do first to start our campaign to prove we're not boring or dull?"

The Comte, who looked pleased to be asked for his advice, appeared to consider for several minutes before responding. Then he pulled a small black leather notebook from one of his pockets, opened it and quickly perused several pages. "Ah," he said, his finger running down a page. "Voilà! The perfect place. There is a shop I want you to go to. The Happy Humping. There they have all the latest toys and gadgets. Not to mention the books and the videos. Also, I understand, the candy and the chocolate. Alas no blood. Yet."

"Happy Humping?" Darlene asked, her voice squeaking. "That place is all about...*sex*." She choked on the last word.

"*Exactement.* The sex. The excitement. A clear and distinct way to quickly prove your unsuitability for the award. After all, to throw the committee off your trail you two will have to present unassailable evidences that you participate in fascinating activities—that you are, as they say, *with it*."

For the first time all evening, Lynette smiled. She'd been after Darlene, the mushy romance queen, to go to Happy Humping for years. That was just the sort of inspiration they both needed to give their writing an edge. But Darlene always refused, finding the idea of a sex shop *unromantic*. Lynette could have gone alone, but she'd known Darlene would never believe what she didn't see with her own eyes. And hadn't Darlene always refused to look at any of the erotic toys they could have ordered from websites?

But now Darlene had run out of excuses. There was no way she could say no to a direct order from the Comte. And Lynette knew that whatever they found at Happy Humping couldn't help but improve their writing for the market. Maybe she'd finally be able to liberate Darlene from her penchant for sappy sentimental love stories and fill their work with ideas based on the hard, sexy stuff they'd find at the shop. Not to mention the possibility of really getting some excitement into their lives…

"We'll do it," both women announced simultaneously. And then they turned to each other and shrugged.

"*Bien sûr*, you will," the Comte said, rising from the couch. "Of course you will. I also recommend to you the Club Decadent for a bit of social life and entertainment. You will go there also. And then you will send me the proof of your new, exciting life so I can inform the committee."

"But Monsieur le Comte," Darlene protested. "How can we possibly attend such a place as this Club Decadent?"

"What do you mean?" he asked, starting to look exasperated.

"In view of our, uh, specialized dietary needs and all," Darlene said in a little voice.

He looked from one to the other of them. "*Mon Dieu*. Did I fail to teach better than that? Do you seriously not know how to comport yourself in such an establishment?"

"She knows," Lynette said. "We both know. She's just gotten flustered, what with your visit and all." Lynette gave her friend a rampaging-vampire glare in warning to keep her mouth shut.

"At any rate, you needn't worry about meeting your needs there. The Club Decadent caters to a unique population. To enter you must tell the guard this secret password."

"I've always wanted to go somewhere that requires a password," Lynette said. "So glamorous. Like spies."

"What if we forget the word?" Darlene asked, chewing her lip.

Lynette glared at her. "I won't forget the word. Uh, what is it, Monsieur le Comte?"

"Geometry.'"

"Geometry?" Lynette repeated. "How am I supposed to remember that?"

"Be there or be square."

"You're kidding." Lynette inwardly groaned. She quite well knew that the Comte never kidded.

He appeared to be growing tired of their company. "You will begin with the wardrobe and the *toilette*. Go to a beauty spa, whatever you need. I am leaving you ten thousand dollars to start. Inform me immediately of any additional expenses you incur."

"This is most generous of you, Monsieur le Comte," Darlene said, practically curtsying again.

"*Mais oui*." He waved off her thanks with a shrug. "And now I must depart. I have made exact arrangements for my return to France."

He then strode through their door and out into the dark shadows.

* * * * *

Darlene couldn't believe that the Comte had voyaged to their home. She'd never, in her wildest dreams, imagined that he'd ever travel to be with them. Of course, the motive for the visit was not a happy one. Imagine that she and Lynette were up for this terrible award. She shivered. And now, to avoid bringing dishonor to the Comte, she and Lynette would have to turn their existences upside down, disrupt their comfort. The Comte demanded they go to that Happy Humping place. Eeew. She'd heard about all the nasty kinds of things they sold there. Stores like Happy Humping glorified sex and trampled over romance.

Well, she'd go to that place to satisfy the Comte and, she hoped, make Lynette and herself ineligible for the nasty award. Then they wouldn't have to worry about being in such a vulnerable situation for another two centuries.

Lynette seemed to think that examining the products at the Happy Humping place—she called it *doing research*—would help them sell their manuscripts. Darlene wasn't about to compromise there. She wanted to keep her love stories free from all that erotic stuff. Their first few books had done quite well on the strength of their insider vampire knowledge. With this last manuscript, Lynette worried that they were repeating themselves. Darlene disagreed. Since their editor echoed Lynette in her rejection, Darlene now had to take those worries more seriously. But there were other directions to take besides a plunge into the erotic, weren't there?

Following the sound of Lynette's impatient holler, Darlene made her way up the stairs to Lynette's bedroom. Once there, she found her friend had pulled all her clothes from her closet and strewn them haphazardly across her open coffin.

"What are you doing?" Darlene asked.

"I'm going through my wardrobe. Figure there's got to be something I can wear that's not made of velour or sweatshirt material." Lynette held up a pair of acid green and orange paisley bellbottoms.

"You're not going to wear those, are you?" Darlene searched her memory for a time when her friend would have worn anything that glaring and atrocious.

Lynette rolled her eyes. "I'd need massive liposuction on my belly, rear, and thighs to even get into them."

"Can we even have liposuction?" Darlene asked.

"Why not?" Lynette hurled the pants into a rather large pile of to-be-discarded clothes. "Maybe I should try to win one of those total body makeovers. Get rid of all the excess."

"You're not fat," Darlene insisted. "Why are you going through your closet now?"

"I'm not going to Club Decadent tonight dressed like a sloppy soccer mom."

"You want to go there tonight?"

"Might as well get started," Lynette said.

"But the Comte said we should go to a spa first."

"You're just trying to delay the inevitable," Lynette accused, pulling out what looked like a black velvet caftan and shaking it, releasing small clouds of dust.

"That looks…interesting." Darlene tried not to cough.

"Not too bad." Lynette examined the caftan more carefully. "I think this might just do for tonight. And I'm sure it will fit."

"I don't remember when you got this."

"Neither do I. Let's check out your closet. It's not even midnight yet. We can still go to the club and scope things out."

Darlene was able to squeeze into a red polyester skirt and tunic. A bit tight across the tummy and the derrière, but she'd be able to sit. Just.

* * * * *

An hour and a short cab ride later, Lynette looked straight at the burly guard stationed at the door to Club Decadent and said, "Geometry."

He replied, "Be there or be square," and waved them in.

A young wolfish-looking man escorted Lynette and Darlene to a small round table in the darkened main room. "Your server will be here shortly for your order," he assured them. Both friends sat so they could easily watch an illuminated circle in the middle of the room.

A woman whose black dress was shorter than her flaming red hair announced that the next show was about to begin.

"Looks like we've arrived just in time," Lynette said. Darlene looked less than thrilled.

To the accompaniment of some very subtle flute and drum music, a young woman with long blonde hair glided into the middle of the circle. She wore a black silk camisole that did little to contain her large breasts, and a black silk thong that barely covered her pussy.

The woman started to dance, looking as if she was searching for someone or something. After several moments, she abandoned her search and ran her hands up her inner thighs several times. Always in time to the insistent beat of the music, the woman began to slip the fingers of one hand in and out of the patch of silk over her pussy, each time leaving her fingers there a little longer and moving her hips more insistently. With her other hand, she resumed her search.

At the least, the woman was a talented dancer — quite beautiful and in fabulous shape. Lynette bit her lip, suppressing a laugh as she watched her friend's reactions. Darlene's eyebrows had disappeared, probably somewhere in her hairline. She'd look at the dancer, then away, then back. Lynette wondered if Darlene would actually sit through the whole performance — which, she thought, was on the tame side for a place named Club Decadent.

But just then a man — obviously the one the dancer had been searching for — came out and embraced her from behind. He was as beautiful and fit as his partner, all rippling muscles and smooth, delicious-looking flesh. His mahogany skin gleamed in the darkness, and his black hair, shorn close to his scalp, contrasted dramatically with the blonde's long mane. He held her tight against him, rubbing his cock up and down her butt — always in time to the music.

Darlene kept forgetting to look away. Lynette snickered to herself, then turned her attention to the twosome. The black man stepped away from the woman, revealing a huge erection that some small scraps of fabric did little to hide. A rush of heat arrowed down Lynette's groin, bringing her clit out of hibernation. She pressed her legs together and savored the friction she was able to produce rubbing her legs together over her long-neglected mound. Why had she let so much time go by since she'd made love — or even just had down and dirty sex? Had her last affair, if her night in bed with a vampire from Berkeley even merited that name, been enough to sour her for — what was it? — ten years? Crazy to let one creep have so much power over her.

But she'd think about all that later. Now her eyes were riveted as the man locked the woman in his arms for a very deep kiss. He slipped his fingers into her pussy, and she returned the favor, circling her fingers around his cock. The man closed his eyes and began to move back and forth, rhythmically. Judging from the blonde's face, he was also doing some magic with his fingertips. Lynette began to breathe harder. Darlene had her hand over her eyes, but this meant little in light of her X-ray vision.

The man drew his fingers, glistening with the blonde's juices, from her pussy to his mouth and sucked. Lynette pressed her legs together and began her own rhythmic movements. She wished she could be where the blonde was now, with her hand around the man's huge cock. Her fingers tingled from remembered contact. The blonde now pulled down the man's scrap of fabric, freeing his cock for them all to feast their eyes on. He relieved her of her thong, revealing her plump, clean-shaven mound.

The two embraced again, their hands racing feverishly up and down each other's backs. The music sped up, and the two were locked in the dance — writhing against each other. Lynette couldn't help herself. The room was dark enough, and anyway everyone's eyes were focused on the couple. She reached under the table and put her fingers where they could do the most good.

Her pussy grew moist with long-dormant desire. Falling into rhythm with the performers, Lynette became reacquainted with her clit and her hungry mound.

The woman kissed her way down the man's sculpted pecs and, getting to her knees, took his gorgeous cock into her mouth. Clutching her head in his hands, and with his own head thrown back and his eyes shut, the man rhythmically moved his ass back and forth. She sucked, bit, licked his cock. With one hand around his butt, she used the other to play with his balls. She slid her mouth to the end of his cock, tonguing the head—and then she took his balls in her mouth and circled his cock with her fingers. Lynette licked her lips. She could just imagine her mouth where the blonde's was. Too much. Her fangs descended, and she had to plant her feet on the ground hard to keep from leaping into the circle and feasting on the man. Her clit began to throb, and Lynette shifted her focus from one hunger to the other.

The man moaned loudly—the first sound he'd made—startling Lynette and the other viewers. Lynette had never before considered herself a Peeping Tom, but now she could definitely see the attraction. Heat emanated from her pussy, swallowing up the fingers she was rubbing herself with. She could feel herself at the brink of a climax and had to bite her lip to keep from screaming out.

The man abruptly pulled away from the blonde—and spurted his cum into the air. Lynette began to vibrate with her own come, relieved for the moment to release her tension. But what about the blonde? Surely they weren't done yet, were they?

The music switched to another tune with the same insistent beat. Another man, a naked white man whose coloring matched the blonde's, came out while the black man and the white woman embraced tightly. The white man began kissing the woman's back and running his hands up and down her sides.

Good, Lynette thought. The blonde was now going to have two men to bring her to satisfaction. Darlene looked on the verge of being sick. Lynette got hot again just thinking about having two men at once. Despite her very recent orgasm, Lynette became aroused again.

The black man began to trace a path down the woman's front, starting at her forehead, moving down, down, covering her with kisses as she held his head. When he arrived at her breasts, he suckled first one, then the other, making slurping sounds. When he released one nipple, the woman used her thumb and forefinger to stimulate herself. At the same time, the white man followed a parallel path on the woman's back. He kept his arms around her waist while he kissed, licked, and nibbled his way down. He paused at her butt, where he tongued and massaged the crack. All the time, the woman swayed to the music and filled the air with her moans. The men arrived at the blonde's feet within seconds of each other. Each stepped back, and she turned around. Now she began to kiss the white man. The black man, hugely erect again, ran his cock across her butt.

"The characters in our books would never do anything so disgusting," Darlene leaned over and whispered. Lynette and several of the nearby patrons shushed her. Lynette's whole hand was now firmly in her panties, and she squirmed with her unfulfilled needs.

Both men now stood apart from the woman. The white man appeared to have nine inches of solid cock, the black man ten. The woman looked from one to the other, then stuck her finger into her pussy, rubbed it down the slit, and brought it out—gleaming wet. The men embraced, their mouths locking as the woman hugged the white man from behind and laid her head on his shoulder.

"Is she going to take both men in her?" Darlene asked, sounding horrified.

"Just watch," Lynette hissed, almost resenting Darlene for distracting her.

The men got down on the floor in what Lynette knew was called a sixty-nine position. They took each other's cocks in their mouths and began to suck and lick. The white man fondled the black man's balls with his fingers. The woman watched, rubbing her pussy, arching her hips over her fingers. Lynette was moving right there with her. The men were beautiful to watch, both looking like a fine artist's creations come to life.

But what about the blonde? Lynette wondered. After all, the black man had come once already. Now it looked like both men were going to come—leaving the blonde to her own devices. Like having your nose pressed against the blood bank window. Joy was so close, and yet so far…

But the men didn't come just yet. Instead, hugely erect and slick with fluids, they drew apart and stood up. The blonde now danced over to them, and ran her tongue down one man's torso, then the other's. She writhed her way down to the floor, where the white man straddled her, his head turned to her pussy.

On his hands and knees, the white man bent his head down to begin licking and nibbling the woman's pussy. The woman moved with abandon, holding her lover's head tightly to where she wanted him. The white man now had his butt in the air. The black man licked his crack, then inserted a finger. The white men swiveled his ass, and the black man removed his finger and, cock fully erect, entered his companion. Lynette quivered with her need. The music grew softer. The black man moved very slowly, his cock sliding in and out of the white man's ass. The blonde rose slightly, took the white man's cock into her mouth, and began to suck. The two of them gyrated to the music and the beat of their impromptu snack. The black man groaned, providing the only words to the music as his two companions had their mouths full. The threesome fell into a rhythm as well coordinated as a minuet.

Watching the white woman arch her pussy against her lover's mouth kicked Lynette into high gear. Her heart raced and her legs began to twitch so hard with her increased desire, she was afraid people would suspect an earthquake. But all too soon, it was clear nothing she could do for herself would suffice. Hell, she needed to get laid, really laid, by some stud as well-endowed as the two now performing.

Darlene, on the other hand, had covered her eyes with her hands. No wonder the two of them were up for that disgusting award—not to mention their big fat rejection. Lynette wanted to grab Darlene's hands away from her eyes and get her to wake up and smell the musk. On second thought, if Darlene kept her eyes covered, she'd never know what Lynette was doing with her hands. It was so dark, and no one was paying any attention to her. Sighing with relief over the blessings of anonymity, Lynette began to ride her fingers.

So hot she could feel steam rising all around her, Lynette couldn't tear her eyes from the sexy threesome, or her fingers from her pussy. The black man stepped backward and removed his big, hard cock from the white man's ass. Lynette swallowed hard as she imagined that hard cock plunging deep inside her. She'd ride him, savoring the sensuous slide of each ridge and vein up and down her wet sheath. He ejaculated a shower of gleaming droplets on the white man's back, and Lynette pressed her fingers tighter into her slick folds.

The white man, his eyes closed and his face looking dreamy, pulled his cock from the woman's mouth. Lynette mirrored the woman as both licked their lips. The white man laid his cock on the woman's chin and spasmed with his release. The woman and man massaged his cum into her face, and Lynette rubbed her clit in time to their rhythm. The white man then took the woman's hand, stood her up, got on his knees, and buried his face in her pussy. Lynette groaned out loud, just imagining the feel of his tongue licking her throbbing clit.

The black man joined them, creating a human sandwich by kneeling behind the woman, who now held the white man's head in her hands, running her fingers through his hair as she writhed and bucked to movement of his tongue. The black man nosed into her butt, licking and fingering the crack. Lynette put one hand on her own ass while she went deeper and harder with her fingers into her pussy. In a short time, the woman arched and heaved against the mouths of both lovers, before groaning out a loud, dramatic release. Lynette, still constrained to silence, was right with the performers. Her lips clamped tight as she shook with the intensity of her orgasm.

The threesome then stood and bowed to loud applause, including Lynette's, before skittering off through an opening in the tables. Darlene still had her hand over her eyes. "You can look now," Lynette hissed. From the way Darlene was behaving, she feared getting out of their current troubles would be an uphill battle.

The lights came on, and their server came to take their order. "Do you have a blood menu?" Darlene asked shyly.

"Of course," the server said. "Just tell me what you want."

"I'll have a B positive cocktail," Darlene said.

"Right." The server repeated her order into a small mike clipped to his collar. "And for you?" He turned to Lynette.

"Hmm. Maybe a bat-and-wolfatini," Lynette said, really determined to have something she'd never get at home. The server left.

"Yuck," Darlene said.

"Hey, I'm not commenting on your order," Lynette said. "Leave mine alone."

"I wasn't commenting on your drink," Darlene said. "But those three people."

"What was wrong with them? It's not like you actually watched."

"Come on, Lynette. I couldn't hide from everything as much as I wanted to. Where was the romance?"

Lynette shook her head. "Exactly. No flowery romance, no sickening sentiment. Just hot sex. Exactly what our characters need." And us, she added to herself.

Darlene put her hands over her heart. "Don't let our heroine hear you say that. You know she's a romantic."

"I disagree. What I know is *you're* too sentimental. And worse, somehow you got the idea that sex is not romantic. Now poor Veronica Vampira's horny as hell— not to mention boring the readers. It's time we expanded her horizons."

"You want her to have sex with two men?" Darlene frowned.

"Why not? That'll get the old juices going." Heck, after what she'd seen, Lynette could go the two men route. Why not the same for Veronica Vampira?

Their server appeared with their orders. "Here's a B positive cocktail for granny number one, and a bat-and-wolfatini for granny number two." He put them down. "I hope you ladies enjoy. I'm Lion. Just let me know if I can get you anything else."

"Did you just call us grannies?" Lynette asked.

"Yes."

"Why?"

He looked her up and down. "You dress just like my grandmother Adelaide."

So much for Lynette's illusion that they could still look hot. Heck, it would have been better to be mistaken as soccer moms than grannies. Lynette controlled her annoyance. But maybe this young idiot was doing them a favor, telling them more honestly than a mirror could have how they appeared. Evidently Veronica wasn't the only one who needed some updating.

"Your grandmother Adelaide come here often?" Lynette asked.

"Yeah. She and her Bingo friends are here once a week."

Great. These days even grannies came to places like Club Decadent. The two of them were so out of it. Lynette was starting to feel the enormity of the task before Darlene and herself. She was also beginning to admit that the possibility of connecting with a stud and getting laid tonight—a hope she hadn't admitted to Darlene—

probably had zero probability of happening. Aside from how good it would feel, she knew in her gut that sending the Comte proof of having a sex life would get her off the short list for the hated award. She took a sip of her bat-and-wolfatini and wished she hadn't. It tasted like swamp swill and burned all the way down. Lynette could see Darlene happily sipping her B. Heck, it was the first time Darlene had stopped frowning since they'd arrived. Lynette knew Darlene would go into an I-told-you-so gloat if she asked her for a sip of the B to get the putrid taste out of her mouth.

Couples were beginning to get up and dance to some very slow saxophone music. Lynette could just imagine herself locked in some big guy's embrace, the two of them swaying minimally to the music as he wedged his erection against her hungry mound. None of the men in the room were coming over to their table to ask them to dance. Lynette was sure Darlene was putting out negative vibes that kept the men away. She regretted not knowing the current etiquette for asking a man to dance. Hell, in a place like Club Decadent, did she really have to worry about rules and all that?

Just then a man came over to their table. Things were looking up. Lynette snuck a peek at him. He navigated himself very well for a man of about a hundred years. He didn't move very quickly, but that was to be expected. He didn't have much hair or any teeth, which became apparent when he opened his mouth to ask Darlene to dance with him.

"I'd be delighted," she said, batting her eyelashes.

Humph, Lynette thought. She took advantage of Darlene's absence to sneak a sip of her B positive, which tasted especially delicious after the shock of the bat-and-wolfatini. She lounged back in her chair to watch the dancers.

Darlene and her senior citizen were locked in an embrace on the dance floor. Lynette suspected that Darlene was providing much of the support needed to keep her partner upright, and she wondered if the old man had much of an erection to press against her friend. Maybe he'd downed a little blue pill earlier... The two of them spent three more dances together before the band switched to a fast song, and the old guy brought a very happy and grinning Darlene back to the table.

"I gave him our phone number," Darlene confided. She picked up her drink and looked suspiciously at Lynette.

"I took a small sip," Lynette admitted.

Darlene scowled, but didn't say anything. She downed the rest of her drink. "Dancing can sure work up a thirst."

"I can't believe you gave that guy our number."

"Cornelius is a sweetie," Darlene said.

"I don't think going out with him will get us off the hook with the bicentennial award committee," Lynette said. "He looks like someone's great-grandfather."

"You're just jealous," Darlene said, looking superior.

Lynette rolled her eyes. "I'm for blowing this joint. I think Happy Humping will be a much better place to get started tomorrow night."

Cornelius was lurching their way again, but Darlene, who mumbled something about following rules and playing hard to get, agreed to leave. They paid their check and headed home. It had, after all, been a big night for both of them. And tomorrow promised to be even bigger.

Chapter Two

From Veronica Vampira's Secret Diaries:
Into the dark, star-filled night I go forth, ever onward in my
relentless search, never losing sight of the most intimate,
personal hopes deep in my tender heart. Where are you, my
charming prince, the one true holder of the golden key that will
release my shattered illusions?

Night fell. Darlene rose from her cocoon-like coffin, though she'd have preferred to stay nestled under her pink and white rose patterned quilt. She couldn't remember the last time she'd spent such a restless day, and now she faced the night ahead with dread. A shudder passed through her as she remembered all that had transpired the night before. The Comte's ominous visit, their editor's harsh rejection...

Dancing with Cornelius had been kind of fun, even though she knew how irritated Lynette had been. Probably jealous 'cause no one asked her. The dance was the only bright spot at that yucky Club Decadent. Darlene scowled. Well, that's what she'd insisted to Lynette all the way home. But secretly she had to admit that watching the threesome had gotten some juices pumping. She did *not* want Lynette to suspect she had any such juices.

After all, Darlene had an image to maintain as somewhat of an innocent. She'd had only one boyfriend before her fateful trip to France with her much more experienced friend. And since that time, there'd been only two short-lived affairs. Of course, Darlene did read a lot. And she had lots of dreams, sexier and more…erotic than she'd ever admit to Lynette.

Despite her snack at the club, Darlene woke up ravenous and, moving practically on autopilot, made her way to the kitchen. She opened the fridge, reluctantly agreeing with Lynette's annoyance when all her eyes lit on was plastic beakers of O positive. That B positive the night before had reawakened slumbering taste buds and sparked a few memories… Maybe it really was time to start getting some variety back in their diet—even if she had to pay full retail.

Lynette stomped into the kitchen dressed in her best black silk and platform shoes that added three inches to her height. She had her hair dressed in a French braid— how'd she manage that? She looked fantastic, in strong contrast to Darlene in her pink flannel Dr. Denton's and coffin hair.

Lynette reached into the fridge for a beaker and made a face. "I'm ready to take all this and dump it down the drain," she muttered.

Darlene gasped. "Waste not, want not."

Lynette put her lips together and produced a large, thankfully dry, raspberry. Despite her complaints, she drank down a full beaker, then a second.

"You're looking glamorous," Darlene said, hoping a compliment might deflect her friend's bad mood.

"You'd better do something to jazz yourself up too. Or did you forget that we're off to Happy Humping? Tonight's when they're opened the latest, so it's our best shot at getting up to speed in the Comte's eyes."

Darlene had been hoping for a quiet night to review their manuscript and think of new, more exciting adventures for Veronica Vampira, and she said so. "Can't we postpone our trip to that place? After all, we did spend hours at Club Decadent last night."

"Which wasn't nearly enough to fix what's broken. You heard the Comte. Not to mention Edna Edmore, our editor. She'd warned us before that our numbers were dropping, that if we didn't put some excitement into Veronica they'd pull the plug. Well, now we've gone beyond warnings. The handwriting is in the big fat rejection. A dull Veronica will be a dead Veronica."

"She's already dead," Darlene couldn't resist saying, though she should have, judging from the fire streaming from Lynette's eyes. "Or undead."

"I mean *really* dead. As in out of print and no longer published."

"Sorry," Darlene said. "I was trying to defuse the tension between us with a little humor."

"It didn't work. Now go get presentable. Do you want me to help you pick something out?"

"I think I can dress myself," Darlene said, leaving the kitchen.

* * * * *

Lynette paced up and down the large kitchen while she waited for Darlene. Lynette rarely spent much time in the kitchen, which was more Darlene's domain. But now she looked around with a critical eye—and she quickly concluded the place really was a dump. She winced, thinking of the elegant Comte. No wonder his face had been pinched in disapproval—as if they'd taken up their homestead in a breeding ground for cockroaches.

Granted, all vampires really required in the kitchen was a fridge to keep the blood fresh. Technically they didn't even need to wash dishes, though she and Darlene did. They had a chipped, permanently soiled sink with a drippy faucet Lynette had trained herself to ignore. A nonfunctioning stove rusted away in one corner, next to a knobless dishwasher. Their cabinets were painted in peeling psychedelic colors. The floor, an ancient black and white linoleum made up of mismatched squares, was cracked, speckled with mouse droppings, and sticky.

In contrast, the Comte had fully equipped restaurant kitchens in his Paris flat and his château in the Loire Valley countryside. High-end crystal, silver, and china gleamed in breakfronts and on the Comte's table. Nary a speck of dust nor a spider web dared to mar the pristine beauty of his walls, windows, and chandeliers. It had been at the château that she and Darlene had fallen under the Comte's spell.

The Comte set a high standard for everything that surrounded him. Somehow, when they'd stumbled into his château, he'd judged them to be at that same high standard—the only reason he'd ever considered transforming them. In retrospect it was clear to her that he misjudged them. They'd arrived fresh from Paris, where they'd snagged designer outfits at bargain prices and perfected their imitations of Audrey Hepburn playing Holly Golightly in *Breakfast at Tiffany's*. They'd managed to fool him then. The way they were now, he'd never even let them in his door as cleaning women.

The Dupont-Monroe Mansion hadn't been in bad shape back in the early 70s, when Lynette inherited it. She and Darlene moved in, then went off to Europe to celebrate. In those days, vampire society existed separate and apart from humans. After their transformation, Lynette and Darlene came up with a tale to explain why they wouldn't be returning to their former lives. When their families got word of their "tragic deaths" in France, Lynette's greedy cousins immediately stepped forward to claim the mansion. She and Darlene, who'd moved back by then, proceeded to "haunt" the mansion—having a ball and permanently scaring off the cousins. Now that vampires and humans mixed more freely, Lynette, put off by her cousins' callous behavior, chose to remain "dead" to them. Darlene, who adored the concept of family, had no known relatives, live or undead.

Lynette and Darlene had planned to fix the old place up again after the cousins' last retreat, but they'd procrastinated. Eventually the mess they'd created and the toll of several decades had turned the formerly elegant mansion into a house of horrors even Halloween party-givers shunned. Unfortunately for the Comte, living in such a dismal abode did little to enhance Lynette and Darlene's status in the vampire community. Well, starting tonight, they were going to change. Maybe along the way they'd restore the place to some of its former glory. But first things first.

"I know it's not as great-looking as what you're wearing, but I think it'll do." Darlene came back to the kitchen looking apologetic—and all wrong in pink ruffled polyester.

"You are not wearing that tonight," Lynette hissed.

Darlene pouted. "It's one of my favorite party dresses."

"You never wore that to a party you went to with me. And you're certainly not going to wear it to Happy Humping. For Pete's sake, you look like the winner of a cookie bakeoff or something. And at this place you're supposed to look like someone who has better things to do with her time than mix walnuts into batter."

Darlene made an I-give-up shrug. "So what do you want me to wear? Do I have to wear black?"

"That would be my first choice. But at the very least no ruffles. And no pink unless it's hot pink. And hurry up. We want to have enough time to really look around when we get there."

Darlene returned in record time wearing a red turtleneck and black leggings. Not perfect, but way better than the pink dress.

Lynette phoned for a cab. A large tan man with a steel-wool beard and white turban showed up at their door ten minutes later. He graciously opened the cab door for them. Lynette slid into the backseat after Darlene. "Where to, ladies?" he asked, his resonant British accent making the simple question sound like a dramatic declamation.

"Happy..." Darlene started saying, when Lynette elbowed her. She didn't know if the driver would recognize the name of the store, but she didn't want to chance any weirded out expressions or comments. So she told him the street address instead.

Both women sat at the edge of their seats during the short trip—and not just because their driver seemed intent on breaking a large number of speed records. Grateful that they were immortal, Lynette tried to relax and focus on what would be the most profitable way for them to spend the coming evening.

The driver pulled up near the front door of the store. "Here you are, ladies," he said, rattling off the address again. Lynette paid him, including a generous tip.

It was close to nine p.m. on this mild evening. Many people still bustled in and out of the small shops on the street. Happy Humping was actually the largest place on the street, with glass display windows on both sides of the double doors.

Both women looked into the store before entering. "There are a lot of people inside." Darlene sounded surprised.

Lynette shrugged. "This place is supposed to be very popular."

"Look, Lynette. There are men in there, too."

"I've heard they're also interested in sex." Lynette opened the door.

"I *know* that," Darlene huffed.

Both of them stood on the threshold for a moment, trying to get their bearings. A crowd of all sorts of people—all shapes, sizes, and ages—filled the shop. Lynette realized she'd expected all the people in a place like this to be young—and mentally slapped herself.

The store was divided into several different sections. Books, magazines, and newspapers lined one long wall. With a pang, Lynette realized that none of their books were among those customers were eagerly perusing. She wanted to change that, to have Veronica Vampira find a niche here.

But the shop sold much more than reading material. One display contained dozens of videos and DVDs spilling over from the counters. Glass cases featured toys, implements, creams, lotions, and potions. Lynette saw candy, chocolate, and other edibles, and she remembered with a pang how much she'd loved chocolate before... For a vampire, the taste of chocolate had no more appeal than wilted celery. Still, the sight of a chocolate penis filled her with several different kinds of longing.

"This is unbelievable," Darlene said, her eyes wide as she and Lynette slowly walked through the store, looking at everything. "I never imagined a place like this existed."

"I've told you about this," Lynette hissed. Now that she was finally here, she regretted waiting this long. You only go around once... Well, that wasn't quite accurate. But maybe the Comte's visit would pull them both out of their inertia.

"I don't understand what all these things are, do you?"

Lynette snorted derisively. "No, that's why we're here. A learning experience. Think about what we can use for Veronica. Not to mention what we'll be able to tell the Comte about."

"Do you really think Veronica would come to a place like this in her quest for true love?" Darlene asked, shock in her voice.

"We're here, aren't we?"

"Yes, but that's different. We're writers doing serious research." Darlene stopped for a moment and walked over to a display of vibrators, all gleaming in jewel and flesh colors. She reached out to touch one, then pulled her hand back as if she'd been burned. "Lynette, whatever you do, don't leave me alone here. Let's stay together."

Lynette rolled her eyes. "What in the heck do you think will happen to you here? You might actually learn something? I think it's a really bad idea for us to stay together. Let's separate, experience whatever we're going to. We can compare notes later."

Darlene screwed up her face. "I don't want to separate. For one thing, we can discuss these various...*things* as we see them, to decide if they'd actually fit in our books."

Lynette's eyes lit up. Darlene had just handed her the key to spending the night the way she wanted. "If we each go around alone, we'll double our exposure to what they've got here. There's way too much to take in at once. Separating will give us twice as many chances to spice Veronica up, right?"

"Yes," Darlene admitted hesitantly. "But let's synchronize our watches. We can come together in one hour to talk about what we've found and plan what to do next."

An hour. Lynette had to admit that was reasonable. "Agreed. Go, try things. Touch. This is a prime chance for us to accomplish what we need to. And don't forget all the money the Comte gave us. If you see something you want, buy it."

Darlene actually blushed, an extremely rare and somewhat painful reaction for a vampire. Lynette worried that Darlene, with her modesty and prudishness, would ruin the night for both of them. Well, they were both on their own for the next hour. Then they'd see what developed.

Lynette saw Darlene head off to look at some books. Though Lynette also wanted to look at books, she purposely headed in another direction so the two of them wouldn't distract each other.

Lynette was curious about all the creams and lotions, finding the variety of containers and flavors exotic and enticing. She picked up a cream that promised to make a man's experience more intense. She bit her lip. Best she could remember, the men she'd been with already found their experience exceedingly intense—not that she was bragging. It had been way too long since she'd been with a man for sex or feeding—or, what she liked best, both. Not since Brad from Berkeley. Bad Brad from Berkeley.

Another cream promised oral sex would be a chocolate and musk delight. Lynette wanted to experience that. There must be a way of including chocolate—and having it pack all the punch chocolate did for humans—in a vampire's diet. That would certainly make immortality a hell of a lot more fun.

Her fleeting minutes would be better spent exploring delights she could actually experience. The dildos were calling her name. Just looking at the array of penis-shaped objects set Lynette's clit to clamoring for some attention. Unlike the night before, she couldn't just slip her hand between her legs and stroke herself to satisfaction. Not here. But she could buy one of the dildos—or more than one—and spend some quality time with it later that night.

The variety of shapes, colors, and sizes aroused her, and her pussy grew moist. Happy Humping provided lots of written information describing the pluses and minuses of the various toys. Vinyl was easier to clean and lighter than rubber. Lynette fantasized about picking various goodies up and trying them out. She suspected that the store personnel, liberal though they were reputed to be, might draw the line at her sampling their products on the sales floor. Too bad. The acrylics looked wonderfully colorful, as did the jelly rubbers. Lynette read that she should use a condom and a lubricant with any dildo, both for safety and comfort. Not being susceptible to pregnancy or infection, she'd never considered condoms a necessity. But for dildo use, they sounded like a good idea.

So she'd buy condoms, too. Maybe fancy, colored, ribbed ones. Fun. But first, a dildo. Though the double-headed ones intrigued her, she'd start with a single.

She rejected the brightly colored jelly rubber one, even though the textures looked yummy, and went with an ordinary black vinyl. As she reached for her selection, a deep voice behind her said, "I was hoping you'd go for one of those."

* * * * *

Darlene looked around at all the people in Happy Humping and hoped they weren't looking back. What must they think of her, being in a place like this alone? She so wished Lynette hadn't just abandoned her. She'd feel far less conspicuous being here with her friend, who had enough chutzpah to carry anything off.

At least Darlene felt safe looking at books, and Happy Humping had a large selection. She could spend her whole hour reading. And then she'd rendezvous with Lynette and they could go home.

The first book Darlene picked up contained lots of photos that reminded her of the so-called show the night before at Club Decadent. Darlene wanted to close the book and put it away quickly, but she had a niggling curiosity…and the strangest tingle deep in her belly. She turned a few pages, using her vampire senses to take in all the pictures at lightning speed. One snagged her imagination… Unbelievable. She put the book back before it corrupted her.

As she felt somehow susceptible to visual images tonight, she reached for a book with no pictures. She picked up a novel, wanting to compare it to her own writing. She read about a beautiful woman, Delecta, who worked at a fancy nightclub and had many men wanting to take her out and buy her expensive gifts. Darlene relaxed a bit. That sounded interesting and romantic, not so different than what she and Lynette wrote—and it was sold in a sex shop. Darlene would tell Edna Edmore about this.

Maybe she and Lynette could have Veronica get a job as a singer in some fancy club. Then Darlene turned the page and found out that Delecta was really a guy named Donald. He went into a lengthy explanation of what he did with his penis when he dressed up… She quickly put the book down.

Maybe she should go over to one of the other displays. That way she'd have something concrete to report to Lynette, who, by the way, wasn't anywhere in sight.

What the heck. Now that she was here, Darlene decided to satisfy a teensy curiosity she'd always had about whips. She couldn't imagine anyone would actually use such things in the name of romance. But some of the various implements were amazingly…well-made. Maybe even beautiful. Created with a fine craftsmanship one wouldn't expect. Fascinating what some people would use their energy to produce…

Her eyes wandered to three types, labeled riding crops, whips, and floggers. The riding crop didn't particularly interest her, but the floggers and the whips caught her fancy. Carefully, she reached over to touch one of the floggers, and instantly jumped back. It wasn't that the flogger had burned her skin or hurt. The moment she'd touched it, she felt a weird stirring down there, at the vee between her legs. Of course if she told Lynette that, Lynette would laugh and call her a wimp. She took a deep breath, stood tall and straight, and let her fingers wander back. Okay, so she got that strange tingling again the moment she made contact. Actually, the tingling felt kind of...nice. As did the warmth spiraling out from that secret place.

Steeling herself, Darlene felt the whip. She stroked the leather tail, and felt like she was stroking herself down there at the same time. Darlene disciplined herself to breathe steadily, to keep her facial expression calm and serene. No one, she convinced herself, could possibly know about the heat and...agitation she felt, especially down there. Not as long as she kept her movements slow and steady, and she kept breathing calmly.

When she felt in control, albeit only on the surface, Darlene looked around. A slightly larger whip called a "braided cat" caught her eye. Darlene serenely put down the flogger and reached over for the elegant object. There appeared to be only one left of this particular beauty, made up of braided thongs. Just as her hand closed around the grip, another hand bumped into hers. A large, hand that gave off electric sparks where it touched her. Darlene gasped and jumped back.

"Don't let me scare you off," a man whispered huskily.

Darlene's eyes grew round as saucers. Scared was exactly how she felt, and she absolutely wanted to run off or dematerialize or something. The thought of doing that here in the middle of the store—and totally freaking out this very good-looking guy and anyone else who happened to see—sufficed to calm her down enough to stay where she was.

"I didn't realize you were reaching for the whip," Darlene said.

"I guess we both have the same great taste." He devoured her with his piercing piratey eyes. I bet you taste amazing, Darlene thought as she gazed into those eyes. So dark they were nearly the blue-black of a midnight sky. Of course not quite as intense as vampire eyes, but amazingly powerful for an ordinary man. An ordinary tall man with thick chestnut hair, a face saved from perfection by a small scar over full, sensuous lips, and a body nurtured on regular workouts. His blood pulsed rapidly and smelled so inviting, Darlene had to bite her lip to keep from puncturing his neck. Despite the O positive she'd quaffed at home, her appetite awoke and howled. As did other hungers.

She shrugged to hide her overwhelming reaction to him. "I was just curious… If you want this, please don't let me stand in your way."

"So how long have you been part of the scene?" he asked.

"Scene? What scene? Did I step into someone's camera shot?" Of course, she knew she wouldn't mess up any photograph, ever. But maybe the photographer had one of those new digital things and would try to figure out why she wasn't showing up. Darlene, flustered, looked around her. What, despite her super-sharp senses and intellect, was she missing?

He smiled at her, and his whole face lit up with devilish glee. "I know it's a line, but...you come here often?"

"My first time," she admitted, and then wondered if she shouldn't have. Lynette was always lecturing her about being cool. Oh well, too late.

"I thought so."

"Really? Why? Because I didn't know what you meant by the word *scene*?"

He chuckled, a sound that sent shivers racing up and down Darlene's spine. "You're quick, and I like that. Not knowing the jargon is a small part of it. Don't worry about not knowing what I meant. I can explain later. You're totally charming."

"Later?" Darlene's heart hammered strangely at the realization that he was trying to pick her up. *Pick her up.* That hadn't happened since college, and not much then...

"Oh, yeah. I'm a people-watcher," he said. "Among my other interests. You see, I'm also an inventor and entrepreneur. Proud to say that Happy Humping sells some of my creations. But all that's for another time. Right now I want to concentrate on you. You're such a fascinating combination of hesitancy and curiosity. I'm glad you've let the curiosity get the upper hand so that you've been checking out the goodies here. I have a strong feeling you're going to let that curiosity lead you to being with me...later."

Darlene laughed to herself at this people-watcher including her among his usual quarry. "So you think you know me after watching for a few minutes?" she asked, not quite batting her lashes, but definitely in flirt mode.

"Not nearly enough." He now stood very near her. "But I'd like to get to know you better. Maybe the two of us could explore why these toys...draw you."

"I just think they're beautifully made. Excellent craftsmanship." Darlene practically chirped. She winced at the sound of her own voice.

"That's all?" He raised one eyebrow, looking amused.

She nodded, catching a poster out of the corner of her eye. "Oh, look. There's a class tonight. 'Whips 101.'" She looked at her watch. "Starts soon. Sounds fascinating. Maybe I'll go, so I won't be such a newbie."

"You could. But I know the teacher. And I promise I could teach you lots more, lots faster...one-on-one."

Whew! Talk about moving fast. If all her instincts didn't tell her he was one hundred percent human male, she'd suspect him of being a vampire or some super masculine type of shape-shifter. A wolf or leopard. She needed to slow things down, so she deflected his question with one of her own.

"And you? Why are you at Happy Humping tonight?"

"To meet you."

She laughed.

"I guess you want more of an answer than that. If I answer your question, maybe you'll stop avoiding mine." His eyes flashed merriment and something darker.

"Let's see," he continued. "I have a lot of respect for this particular business. As you've seen with the whips and other implements you've been looking at, they carry a superior line of products. You wouldn't believe the shoddy garbage some places try to pass off as the real goods."

"So you've bought other...whips and things?" Darlene's interest level kept rising, along, unfortunately, with her voice.

"Oh, yeah," he said, grinning. "I have an extensive personal collection of some of the finest bondage and submission goodies in the city and beyond."

"Really? Why?" she asked.

He gave her a *who do you think you're kidding* look. "Not just for show," he said so softly that she might not have heard him without her superior auditory sense.

Darlene felt goose bumps shiver up and down her arms for the second time since she met him. Delicious goose bumps. Talk about curiosity. Thinking about what this man did with whips and other implements had her pussy in turmoil.

"Then I guess I should just leave the 'braided cat' to you, seeing as how you appear to be a collector and all," Darlene babbled. She needed to get away from this man before she became involved in something she couldn't even imagine. In the writer part of her brain, she made note of her sensations for Veronica's future adventures. Heck, she needed to do whatever she could to distance herself and Veronica from this very dangerous situation.

"It's been pleasant meeting you," she added, starting to move away from him.

"Not so fast." He reached out and grabbed her arm.

* * * * *

"Excuse me." Lynette backed away from the proverbial tall, dark and handsome stranger whose smile was wreaking havoc with her groin.

"Sorry if that sounded abrupt. I'm Nicholas LaStrada. My friends call me Nick."

"Nick," she repeated, considering how well the name fit the man in front of her. Probably thirty-five or so. Thick black hair worn on the long side, and black eyes that snapped with intelligence and wit. A full sensuous mouth beneath a bushy black moustache and teeth that gleamed white when he smiled.

"And your name?" He held out his hand.

"Lynette." Her voice sounded thin and reedy to her ears. "Lynette Loring."

"Pretty name for a pretty lady."

"Thank you," she said, genuinely pleased at his compliment. She shook his hand and nearly flew through the ceiling at the jolt of electricity the contact generated. Looking at him, touching him, Lynette nearly shuddered with horniness and man-hunger.

"Uh, Lynette. I don't mean to sound too personal, and I'm sure not the morality police. But are you really old enough to be shopping here?"

Lynette felt so startled by his question, she didn't answer right away. "How old do I need to be?"

"Eighteen."

She bit her lip. "You think I look like a teenager?"

He considered. "Well, I'd say a college student. Pretty young."

She chuckled. After the waiter at the Club Decadent last night called her a granny, she enjoyed Nick's more flattering perception. "I've been out of college for a while." No sense giving him too much information…

"Well, you could pass for a coed. Easy. So, you gonna buy that?" he asked.

"I might." She fingered the dildo while he watched, and wondered what he was thinking.

"How about if I treat you to it and some other goodies, and then we go out for a drink?"

"No, I'm going to buy this," she said, dodging the invitation. "All the things I'm looking at tonight are part of my research—as a writer."

He looked impressed. "So what do you write? Do they sell any of your books here?"

"Not yet," she said. "What other goodies should go with this?"

"Condoms—and a harness. Also lubricating cream."

"You sound like a man of experience." She firmly held onto the dildo as the two of them went over to the condoms display.

She'd have gladly bypassed the dildo for a romp in bed with Nick. But then a memory flashed through her. The time when she was still human and went to bed with a gorgeous hunk who tried to convince her beforehand that size didn't matter. Turned out that, fully erect, his cock had less to offer than his pinky. He mounted her and entered her, and all she felt were his hips thrusting against hers. Adding insult to injury was his name—Dick.

Dick hadn't been quite as good-looking as Nick, but almost. And here this Nick was hanging out at the dildos section of Happy Humping. That had to tell her something. Maybe Nick didn't have much to offer either. Clearly he appeared to want to get her and a dildo to leave the store with him. With bed in mind?

Well, Lynette had hoped for some experiences she could pass on to Veronica—and, of course, enjoy herself. Hey, she was no martyr to her art. Nick might hold the key to raising Veronica's print run. He certainly had a lot more going for him than Cornelius, the old codger who danced with Darlene last night.

Darlene. Lynette couldn't just abandon her friend here. Not that Darlene couldn't get home on her own. But there was something in the old high school code about not leaving your girlfriend stranded to go off with some guy... Amazing that she still remembered all that crap.

"These are top of the line," Nick held up some samples of nearly sheer condoms.

Lynette admired them before her glance took in the price tag—and she nearly shrieked. Those suckers cost enough to be made of spun gold. And that was only a slight exaggeration. "You think they're worth it?" She tried to sound cool.

"Can't say. Haven't tried 'em. What did you have in mind?"

"I thought maybe ribbed, textured. Less expensive." She tossed the words off nonchalantly.

"Hmm. You mean like these?" He held up a packet that was considerably more reasonably priced.

"Yeah. They sound...interesting." She took the package of three from him and picked up two more.

"Optimistic, aren't you?" he asked, his eyes twinkling.

"I don't get here often."

"They do have a catalog."

"This is more fun. So Nick, what else do you suggest?"

He promptly answered, "A harness."

He'd mentioned that before. "Show me."

He once again led her directly to the right place. "Voilà!" Damn, he really knew his way around this shop.

She hated to seem naïve, but she really couldn't figure out how she—or Veronica—would use the harness. But she already felt comfortable enough with Nick to ask.

He gazed at her with a hooded sexy look. "Come out for a drink and I'll tell you all about it. Even draw you a picture if you'd like."

Lynette wanted to go out with him from the moment she saw him. Now she began thinking about how to take him up on his invitation. "Uh, I'm actually here with a friend."

"Really? A girl friend or a guy?" Nick looked mildly concerned.

"My best friend Darlene."

"Invite her with us."

Lynette felt a flutter of disappointment. So he didn't want to be alone with her after all. She figured Darlene would never go for leaving anywhere with Nick, but she'd ask. They went off in search of her.

* * * * *

"I have a proposition for you," the mysterious stranger said to Darlene. "Seeing as how I honestly believe chivalry's not dead, how about if I let you buy the whip—on one condition."

"What condition?" Darlene asked hoarsely.

"Come home with me. I want to show you a new DVD I'm buying." He held up a package where a hooded man brandished a whip over a naked woman straddling the chair she was tied to. "As an intro to the world of the whip. I'm quite sure you'll find a lot to enjoy."

"Home with you?" Darlene asked, nearly dying of curiosity and desire. She felt like she'd come to a new awareness since she started talking to this man—a man whose name she didn't even know. So how could she logically feel that she was in for the romantic evening she'd been dreaming of for years?

"Yes, come home with me to my palace of delights. Or, in this case, condo. By the way, fair lady, my name is Jon Torrance. And you?"

Jon. His name was Jon Torrance. "Darlene DeMars."

"Pleased to meet you, Darlene DeMars. Come home with me."

"I can't." She regretted those words as she said them.

"Why not?"

"I'm here with my friend, Lynette."

"The two of you are joined at the hip?"

"It's not that," Darlene said.

Just then, Lynette came up to her. Darlene nearly sighed with relief. Jon represented such danger. Lynette would rescue her, return her to sanity.

Except that Lynette wasn't alone… A large man with black hair and a mustache followed right behind her, hands full of packages.

"Darlene, I'd like to introduce you to Nick LaStrada. Nick, this is my best friend, Darlene DeMars." Lynette's chin jutted out with determination.

Darlene couldn't believe it. Lynette also met a gorgeous guy? Talk about a place that had everything.

"Darlene, Nick and I would like to go out for a drink. Would you like to come with us? Or would you mind going home alone if you don't want to go?" Darlene could see in Lynette's eyes how much her friend wanted to go out with this man.

What a strange and amazing coincidence. "Lynette, I have someone to introduce *you* to. This is Jon Torrance. And he's invited me to his condo to see a video."

"To his condo for a video?" Lynette echoed.

Darlene nodded.

"And you're considering going?" Lynette's voice rose in surprise.

"I'd like to, if that's all right with you," Darlene said, thrilled at how everything was falling into place. For the first time since the Comte's visit, she was beginning to feel happy.

"Is it *ever* all right with me." Lynette turned to Nick and gave him a thumbs-up.

She turned back and said to Darlene, "Don't forget to be home before dawn."

"Of course. And you, too."

Both men laughed. "I promise to get her home on time," Nick said to Darlene.

Each couple briefly eyed the other's goodies. Then they all paid for their booty and headed out for their separate adventures.

Chapter Three

From Veronica Vampira's Secret Diaries:
Love, true blue, rare as the most delicate blossom blooming on a
snowy mountain peak at midnight, love is the almighty
alchemical elixir, the inebriating intoxicant I desperately long to
imbibe from the running, gurgling, babbling waters of life…

"We can go for a drink at a place near Happy Humping," Nick said to Lynette once they were out on the street. He insisted on carrying her package. "It's such a nice night, let's walk."

"Sounds good to me." Lynette savored the sights and sounds of the still busy street. What with the Internet and the pattern—or rut—she'd fallen into, she really hadn't gotten out much in a long time. Though she hadn't expected to be grateful to the Comte for much of anything after last night, now she mentally thanked him.

Like most other vampires, Lynette didn't drink alcohol. Many people had the misconception that vampires *couldn't* drink alcohol. Vampires could eat and drink anything other beings did. But most vampires preferred blood, which was exquisitely suited to their delicate palates and their bodily needs…and tasted best.

"Here we are, my lady," Nick said when they arrived at a place called Creatures of the Night. When she read the name of the bar, she wondered if Nick knew a lot more about her than he was letting on. Though a small population of vampires inhabited San Francisco, most humans didn't recognize vamps in the normal course of events. Especially now that the easy availability of blood for purchase meant vampires no longer relied solely on feeding from live creatures. Most vampires chose to maintain a low profile, as some intolerance toward their kind still persisted.

"Is this one of your favorite haunts?" she asked, taking in the dark décor. The bar owner favored fake spiders and their webs, ghoulish specters, and elegant vampires with exaggerated teeth and chalk-white skin.

"Haunts? Oh, you mean because of the name. Good one," Nick said, chuckling. "I just like this place. I come here after all my trips to Happy Humping."

"And are those often?" she asked as he guided her to a booth in the darkest and most obscure corner of the small, nearly empty bar.

"Not that often, though I get a real kick out of that shop."

Lynette eased herself in across from him, admiring the angles and planes of his face in the flickering light from a fat white votive candle in a red holder. "And tell me, Nick. Do you always pick up women there and bring them here?"

He crossed his artistic long-fingered hands over his heart and looked wounded. "Lynette, this is the first time ever. Usually I just hang out at the shop for a while, get a drink, and go home. I never even notice the other people there. But I saw you, and right away I realized there was something special and different about you. And that I wanted to get to know you."

"That means you 'got lucky' tonight?" Lynette could hear the sarcasm in her voice as she used the old cliché.

"Oh, yeah." And then he probably realized she was pulling his chain. "I don't mean it the way people usually do when they say 'got lucky'."

"What do you mean, Nick?"

"That I feel really fortunate to have met a great young lady who's willing to spend time with me."

Nick's sincerity touched Lynette, piercing her habitual cynicism. He reached across and began stroking the palm of her hand in an amazingly sensuous pattern. Lynette had never before realized the direct link between her lifeline and her clit. Based on his confident gaze, Lynette concluded Nick knew exactly what effect he had on her. She wiggled her legs together surreptitiously to ease some of the tension rising from her pussy. Was he sporting a huge erection under the table? Lynette didn't want to stare too blatantly, and the shadows kept Nick's groin shrouded...

She wondered again if Nick's interest in dildos stemmed from a lack of equipment. For a moment she lost herself in a fantasy of being in bed with an incredibly hard Nick. It would just be too cruel a trick of nature if a gorgeous guy like him didn't have the follow through to follow through... Her gut told her she'd find out before she returned to her coffin at dawn.

"What can I get you to drink?"

Your neck, she thought. She mentally slapped down her vampire appetite, switching to proper dating behavior. "Wine."

"Red or white?"

"Red. Merlot."

"Be right back." He got up and headed for the bar.

Lynette feasted her eyes on Nick's butt as he smoothly sauntered over to the bar.

* * * * *

Why had he picked Lynette up? Nick asked himself while he went to the bar to order the drinks. She sure wasn't his usual type. He tended to go for size four blondes in designer clothes with legs up to their chins. He laughed dryly to himself. Yeah, he usually preferred the barracuda type who'd suck him dry before going on to the next guy with the bigger stock portfolio.

The kind who were good for a fuck as long as it didn't mess up their hair. That is, the hair on their heads. Usually had a Brazilian down below. His cock stirred at that thought.

Though he didn't know exactly how old Lynette was, he believed her that she was older than she looked. She had the kind of youthful good looks that stayed with people forever. With her black hair in a haphazard bun and her large brown eyes, pert nose, full red lips, and a body that testified to no time spent in a gym, she didn't seem particularly up on fashion or interested in Wall Street. If he mentioned the word, Lynette would probably think a Brazilian was a soccer player if he mentioned the word. But—and he didn't understand why—that didn't matter. For some reason, tonight she *felt* exactly like the right woman for him. His cock voted yes.

* * * * *

He returned with her red wine in one hand and a mug of beer in the other. As for his crotch—well, the zipper tented out with great promise.

Of course, he could have bought a pants-stuffer or crotch enhancer at Happy Humping. Heck, he could have some tissues crammed in his pants. But her instincts told her that Nick wasn't the type to go in for false advertising. Not unless he was a hell of an actor and all the sincerity she was picking up was a sham.

Nick put the drinks down. "You want some pretzels or nuts?"

The only nuts she wanted were his. "Just the drink's fine."

"I'm not hungry either," he said. "For food."

Probably the corniest line in the universe, but coming from Nick LaStrada, it worked. He proposed a toast. "To a very special night."

"I'll drink to that." She raised her glass. Her fangs began to descend, and she had to concentrate on retracting them before she began to drink. Didn't want to freak Nick out.

Nick took a large swallow of beer and set his mug down. "So, tell me about yourself, Lynette. What's a pretty girl like you doing at a place like that?"

She couldn't not roll her eyes. "Do you really get anywhere with lines like that?"

He laughed. "You'd be surprised."

"I guess. Well, okay. I'll treat that like a real question. The short answer is that I was really there to do research with Darlene, who's my best friend, housemate, and writing partner."

He looked intrigued. "Housemates? Are you two a couple?"

"Would it bother you?" she asked, amused.

"Hey, it's San Francisco. I guess what I'm asking is if you're a monogamous couple, only into women?"

She laughed, making sure to keep her lips closed around her fangs. Damn, she wished they'd retract. But whenever she got in any way excited, they came out. "No to all your questions. Darlene's been my best friend since high school. After college, we started writing together. When I inherited a large house here in the city, with real estate costing what it does, it just made sense for us to move in together."

"So you really have graduated from college. It can't have been long ago."

Lynette did not want to go into detail here. "Time flies when you're having fun."

"Uh, yeah. Say, is that wine okay? You don't seem to be drinking much."

"It's fine. You're not trying to get me drunk or something, are you?"

"Busted. No, just kidding. I like my women awake and aware."

"Which is how I like to be. Nursing my drink very slowly keeps me that way."

"So tell me about what you and Darlene write." He took another swallow of his beer. "Have I heard of any of your books?"

"Probably not. But I've talked enough. I want to hear about you, and why you were hanging out at Happy Humping tonight."

"You got it." He took another swig of beer before he began.

"Let's see. Nick LaStrada. Single, native San Franciscan. Went as far afield as Berkeley for college," he chuckled dryly. "Lord, that makes me sound insular, and I'm not. I travel lots for the family business, and I love seeing other places. But San Francisco always has been and will be home."

"What's the family business?"

"Import-export. Fine art and jewelry. Takes me to lots of cities in Europe and Asia, sometimes more than I want to go."

"Sounds fascinating. And lucrative."

"It can be. Both. Do you travel much?"

"Not anymore. I did when I was younger." Lynette's memory flashed to their last trip — to France...

Nick's eyebrows shot up. "Younger? What, when you were five?"

She forced her focus back to the present. Shit, he seemed to be obsessing about her age. She waved her hand dismissively. "I traveled a lot when I was in school. That's all I meant."

"Lynette, I'm dying of curiosity here. How old are you?"

She shrugged. "Age is just a number."

"Mine's thirty-four. Please tell me yours."

Her mind glommed on to the last living birthday she'd had. "Twenty-three. Can we talk about something else?"

"Geez, you're young."

"Trust me on this. I'm a *very* old twenty-three. But about you. You look like a man who enjoys his work."

Nick nodded. "Sometimes, though, work consumes my days and nights. And then it's like I have no life. Which is why I go to hang out at Happy Humping. To remind me to get a life."

"But what is it specifically about that shop? What are you looking for, Nick LaStrada?"

"Good question," he said. "Lynette, I've got this gut instinct that I can be really honest with you. And you won't go screaming into the night."

Lynette wondered where this was leading. How long would it take him to run screaming into the night if she were equally honest with him? "I'm a big girl." She looked at him expectantly.

"I'm working my way up to telling you." He drained off the last of his beer and went to get another drink. He offered to get her something else, but she declined.

Lynette wondered how bad what he was hiding would be. Nick didn't look weird. Quite the contrary. Well, she knew he couldn't hurt her, not unless he was a very competent vampire hunter. But none of her survival instincts were clanging for attention.

She took a sip of her wine and cringed at its thin, lifeless, sour taste. But if she wanted to have a more interesting social life, she had to get used to swallowing the vapid brew without making a face. Or learn to drink something else.

Nick returned with his beer.

"So, you were going to tell me…" she said, her tone cool.

He took a sip of his beer. "I like you, Lynette."

"You don't waste any time, do you?"

He held up his glass and saluted her. "I listen to my instincts." He put down his glass and reached across the table to stroke her face with his fingers. She shivered at his touch. "I like what I've seen and heard so far. And I want to get to know you lots better—soon. Life's too short…"

She raised her eyebrow. "So, aside from your over-reliance on clichés, what's supposed to make me go running out into the night? I like you, too, Nick."

"That's good, real good." He turned his beer mug nervously in his large hands. "Come home with me," he said, his voice just above a whisper.

She leveled her gaze at him. Not her hypnotic, paralyzing vampire death stare. Just her don't-bullshit-me look. "Nick, what aren't you telling me? I'm open to a lot, but I don't like weird surprises. Like maybe going home with you and finding out you're really a woman who gave up on depilatories."

He laughed at that and pushed his mug aside. "I'm all man, and I can't wait to show you."

"I can't wait either."

"If you'll take one shoe off and reach over, I can give you an appetizer." Nick's voice grew very low.

Sounded kinky. Was Nick about to reveal a foot fetish? Her pussy muscles contracted, as she slid her shoe off and raised her foot under the red and white cloth. He instantly enveloped her foot with his two strong hands and positioned it smack on his hard cock. She stepped down firmly and he moaned. "That's all for you, baby. It's solid, it's real, and it's waiting."

Lynette plied him with her foot, getting sensuously turned on. Even her fangs throbbed. Damn, she needed to get laid. Soon. And hard. Nick absolutely felt like the real deal. "You don't think a hard cock is going to freak me out, do you?"

"No," Nick said. He closed his eyes and groaned. "Much as I hate to ask you to stop, I'm going to come if you keep that up. And I'm noisy as hell when I come."

That might be a lot of fun, but Lynette really didn't want to attract attention. Reluctantly, she pulled her foot away and put her shoe back on. None of which stopped her pussy's clamoring.

"...your fantasies?" he asked.

"Sorry. I missed the beginning of what you said."

He winked. "I asked what your fantasies are. Or, is there one fantasy you're just panting to try out—and you've never been able to?"

Lynette wrinkled her brow. Fantasies... She couldn't come up with any. "For now, I'd rather listen to yours," she said, containing her fangs in what she hoped was a sultry grin.

He exhaled. "You're really special." He took her hand again.

She rolled her eyes. "What are you taking such a long time to tell me, Nick LaStrada? Out with it."

He took another large swallow of beer. "Lynette, you know about the dildo and the harness?"

"Of course. I just bought them."

"Yeah, well I have a large collection of dildos at home. Also quite a few harnesses."

Now Lynette felt really confused. He didn't need to wear a dildo to make it with her. Then a thought came. "That doesn't mean you're gay, does it?" she asked. When he didn't answer, a second thought flashed into her mind. "No. You're interested in me, so you must be bi."

He shook his head. "I've never been attracted to guys."

"Huh?" she said. "I mean, it would be okay with me if you were — gay or bi or anything else…"

"Yeah, but I'm totally not."

Who was she to get fussy about labels? "Fine. So go ahead, tell me the rest."

Another pause. Then Nick took the plunge. With his eyes large and dark he whispered, "It's about the dildo and harness."

"Spit it out, man."

He nodded once. "I-have-this-desire-to-have-a-woman-fuck-me-up-the-ass-with-a-dildo." He said the whole thing so quickly, it sounded like one long word.

He wanted her to put on a harness and dildo and fuck his butt? That was it? "Cool."

Nick sagged with what Lynette took to be relief. "I've never told anyone that before."

"Glad to be the first," Lynette said.

"Then you'll think about doing it?" Now he looked anxious, as if he'd just asked her to sail an inflatable plastic barge across the Pacific.

Lynette wasn't a game player… End of story. "Sure."

"I never thought it would be this easy." He looked slightly dazed. Lynette shrugged as if she agreed to fuck men in the butt several times a week. Her voice as cool and sophisticated as she could make it, she said, "This is my night for the new and different. One thing, hotshot. I want to get up close and personal with that erection first. You know, the old-fashioned way?"

"Hey, I didn't mean to imply I don't want to do it that way." He was smiling sheepishly.

"Good." Her pussy creamed in anticipation.

"I just want to do it the other way, too... God, if you knew how many years I've been waiting..." He looked earnest and adorable.

"Let's blow this joint." She rose.

Maybe that wasn't all she'd blow tonight. Lots of hours before dawn.

* * * * *

Jon Torrance had described his place as a penthouse, and he wasn't exaggerating. When Darlene walked in, she felt like she'd entered a movie set. Of course he had a gorgeous view of the Golden Gate Bridge and the Bay. Though the view she and Lynette had was almost as good, everything looked a lot more impressive from Jon's penthouse.

"Want something to drink?" Jon asked. "Before I show you my special collection, as promised."

"And the DVD," Darlene said, then wished she could take back the words. She didn't want to sound too pushy.

"Of course. Actually, I have several hundred videos and DVDs to choose from. In addition to the one I just bought. Now that I've given it some more thought, I'm not convinced it's the right one for you for tonight. Seeing as how you're a virgin, I want to make sure to pick one that will get you started right."

"A virgin?" she echoed. Hardly that.

He chuckled huskily. "I meant to this scene. You've never done any bondage and submission before, have you?"

"Guilty as charged," she admitted. She hadn't realized that her gentle exploration of the whips had anything to do with bondage or submission. Heck, maybe she really was as naïve as Lynette said. Now that she was with a movie-star handsome man who seemed to know his way around the "scene", she had to admit that more than her curiosity was aroused. Much as she wanted to believe she was just doing Veronica research, she was nearly breathless anticipating what would happen next. To Darlene, not to Veronica.

The penthouse was huge and gorgeous. Darlene thought about how rundown the home she shared with Lynette had become. Jon led her into a large entertainment room that contained state-of-the-art audio and video equipment housed in ebony wood and glass cabinets. Black leather couches and ebony tables sat on marble floors, all shown to advantage under recessed lighting. A huge statue of a naked man entwined with a woman stood in front of the window. Darlene looked around at the many works of art—lithographs, sculptures, huge framed photographs, an oil painting—arranged with care around the room. She wanted to examine each piece, but she suspected she had much more ahead of her before she returned home by dawn.

"Would you like to see my collections first or watch the DVD?" Jon asked.

"You have more than one collection?"

"Doesn't everyone?"

"Definitely the collections first," Darlene said.

"Good choice." Jon took her by the elbow and steered her over to one of the ebony cabinets.

"I have some of my whips, cats, and floggers in this cabinet." Jon carefully turned the handle on one door.

"Just some of them?" Darlene asked, surprised. Jon was opening a large cabinet.

"Yeah. My collection outgrew this cabinet, so I've expanded into my bedroom."

"I guess they're handy there," Darlene said with false bravado. Was she ever in over her head. She tried to identify her feelings so she could write them into a Veronica story. Darlene laughed to herself. There was no way Lynette could top what she was doing tonight. What would Lynette say when Darlene told her about Jon Torrance's whips and toys? She wouldn't admit to Lynette how damp her panties were, and how Jon made her body tingle with his words and his touch

"Would you like to take any of them out and touch them?" Jon indicated the thirty or so implements he had meticulously displayed on shelves in the cabinet.

Darlene looked carefully at everything. "I'd like to touch each one of them," she said, "but I don't think there's enough time tonight. Jon, what were the names you used? Do you mind telling me again?"

He put his hand on her shoulder, jacking her senses up to a higher level. "I love to play teacher. Especially to such a delightful student. Let's see. The difference between whips and cats and floggers…"

Darlene found everything Jon told her fascinating. She wanted to hold on to all the facts, to have her brain fully engaged. Men loved it when women ate up their words, right? Usually, with her superior vampire intelligence, she'd have had no problem. But some interference was clouding her accustomed clarity. She hadn't felt this unfocused since she was human. What was making her so fuzzy? Could it be Jon—or the unusual night? Or both? Much as she hated to admit it, maybe the Comte had a point.

"The next part of my collection is in my bedroom," he practically whispered in her ear. The sound of his voice set all her nerve endings to anarchy. She wanted to feel his warm breath fan her face, tickle her skin. "Are you okay with going there?"

Darlene successfully stifled a most inappropriate giggle. Did he really think, after everything she'd seen and touched already, that she'd demur at going to his *bedroom*? Aside from her curiosity about it, she knew that her vampire strength would keep her safe from anything she didn't want.

Jon led her down the marble floors of his hallway far too quickly for Darlene to appreciate the art lining the walls on both sides. "How many bedrooms do you have here?"

"Four, but I've found other uses for all but mine, which is the only one with a bed."

"Other uses?" she asked, intrigued.

They now stood at the threshold of his bedroom. "One room is my home office, all my computers and tech equipment. The others…well, I look forward to showing you sometime soon. But first, I'd like to show you the rest of my collection here."

Jon's bedroom amazed Darlene even more. A mirrored ceiling, of course. A king-sized bed, with an ebony-barred headboard and footboard, the mattress and pillows covered in what looked like fine black silk. More paintings and sculptures. At various places on the white walls, different implements jutted into the room. Darlene didn't know where to look first. "You actually sleep in this room?"

"Of course," he said. "Sometimes." He had his hand at the small of her back and steered her over to an enormous ebony wood armoire that took up an entire long wall of the room. A large number of cabinets and chests, and a smaller armoire, all ebony wood, were placed aesthetically around the room.

"This is where I have more of my toys." Jon opened the two massive doors that kept the armoire's contents out of sight.

One section contained what looked like an artistic arrangement of five metal thong undergarments. "What are those?"

"I assume you've heard of chastity belts?"

"I have, but I never knew they existed in this day and age." Darlene's face colored as she once again chastised herself for being so naïve. Fortunately, Jon didn't seem annoyed. "But I've never seen one before. May I touch?"

"Of course."

The shiny metal felt cold to her touch. Darlene wondered what use Jon put his chastity belts to. But before she could ask, the rest of the armoire's contents caught her eye.

"You must have more whips here than Happy Humping," Darlene said, impressed.

"I enjoy growing my collection. I'm always finding new goodies that I can't resist."

"Like the one we both went after tonight?"

He grinned, indicating a brilliant smile. "I consider losing out on that a small price to pay for getting to know you."

Darlene surveyed the more than eighty whips and floggers housed in the beautiful armoire. As before, each was placed meticulously on a shelf that seemed custom-made to show it off.

"You have even more of these elsewhere?"

"Guilty," he answered. "But I don't want to overwhelm you, seeing as you're so new to the scene."

"Thank you for being so thoughtful." Darlene took in the whole display, amazed at how beautiful each item in his collection was. As a vampire, Darlene knew that, despite her surprise at all she saw, nothing he had here would ever overwhelm her.

She suspected Jon, on the other hand, would be freaked out if he knew her true nature. So she had to try to remember what it felt like to be human and on the verge of being overwhelmed. At least for now. She began to play with the idea of really introducing herself to him, wondering what would happen if she misjudged his reaction. Jon seemed unflappable. But would a display of her fangs rattle him—or would he think she was *cool*? Too early to decide.

"Have you used all of these?"

He raised an eyebrow. "I'm never one to kiss and tell."

"You kiss with these?"

"In a manner of speaking. You *are* curious. You sure you're not part cat?"

She considered that for a moment. "I might very well be. Nine lives sounds appealing, especially in light of the penalty for curiosity."

"Good," he said. "Let's get started."

A shiver raced down Darlene's spine. What was he going to show her first?

"Are you ready for that DVD now?"

"Sounds great." Darlene tried to imbue her voice with more enthusiasm than she actually felt. After all, she could watch DVDs at home. But this condo was a treasure trove of far more interesting pastimes... Not to mention, she wanted to do more than just sit next to Jon as images flickered by. "Though I would like to have another look at those chastity belts." Actually, she'd like to see how they worked. But she didn't feel confident to say that.

"That can easily be arranged. Look at anything, often as you want. I have my new DVD player out in the living room." He appeared somewhat impatient, but stood near her as she took a last look around.

The bed beckoned, with its wide expanse of black silk...covering what? Darlene imagined herself in the bed with Jon, and a delicious roiling fanned out from her groin. What would it be like rolling around on that huge mattress with him? He'd probably bring some of his toys into play. Before now, she'd never done anything more exotic than fun and games with a vibrator, and she'd run out of batteries years ago. A tingle caressed her pussy folds.

But they were leaving Jon's bedroom. He was leading her out without making a move. Did that mean she didn't turn him on sexually? With all the equipment in this bedroom, Darlene couldn't believe they wouldn't be able to just climb into his bed and watch a DVD from there.

If Lynette were here, she'd open her mouth. Lynette wouldn't be afraid to ask for what she wanted.

"State-of-the-art video equipment out here," Jon was saying. "I want you to get the clearest possible view of the DVD we're going to see."

Not the opportune moment to tell him about her superb vampire vision.

Jon opened another cabinet to reveal several hundred alphabetized videos and DVDs. "I haven't gotten all the videos on DVD yet. And some of what I have here are classics, perfect for virgins."

"I'm not a..." Darlene was about to repeat, then stopped. After all, he seemed to be getting some sort of kick out of calling her a virgin. Once they got into the sack, she'd show him how totally this name did not describe her.

"I'm torn between these two—both, alas, videos." Jon held up two packages.

"Let's see," Darlene said, reading the titles. "*Alice in Bondageland* or *Lots of Pain, Lots of Gain*." The first showed a young nude woman with numerous ropes tied around her. She was looking soulfully at a hooded, masked man in black leather who had her long blonde hair clenched in his fists. The second showed another hooded, masked man holding a whip over a brunette woman in tattered black lace.

"Which one would you recommend?"

"They're both excellent for newcomers. Educational and all that." Jon put first one then the other up for her closer perusal. "I want you to choose."

Darlene had never heard the word *educational* used exactly like this. "I always liked the Alice stories. So why don't we start with that one?"

"One of my personal favorites." Jon put *Lots of Pain, Lots of Gain* back in its proper slot. "The actress who plays Alice is one of my best buddies."

A flicker of jealousy zigzagged through Darlene. "She's beautiful," she said begrudgingly.

"She is that," he said, with a faraway sound in his voice that made her suspect something more than friendship had existed between the two. Darlene would be very disappointed if all she did tonight was watch a video, no matter how wild. Lynette would probably gloat—and then insist on having her views dominate the next story they wrote about Veronica. "Why don't you make yourself comfortable on the couch while I get this going?"

Darlene sat on the couch and watched as Jon set up the video. She thought he'd start it and sit down with her, maybe do some cuddling as they watched. Instead he said, "I need to get one more thing. Be right back."

* * * * *

Darlene had to be the most naïve adult in San Francisco. Normally, Jon had little patience for dealing with anyone who walked around in openmouthed amazement. Hell, Darlene dressed like a hick, sounded like one, acted like she'd just gotten off the bus from Nebraska or some other Podunk depot. Granted, Darlene was young—looked to be only in her early twenties. A real Alice in Wonderland type, a genuine ingénue. He normally found anyone this "innocent" dull. So why did she get his juices jumping the way she did?

Maybe he'd been getting bored with the same old, same old. Seemed like all the subs he took home shopped at the same boutiques, wore the same makeup. Gorgeous, but starting to get old.

Darlene was a genuine original. But there was something else about her, something under the surface. Maybe he'd get lucky tonight and find out just what that was. There was something very appealing about digging below the surface and actually finding hidden treasure.

And, if, despite his gut instinct, he dug and there really was nothing there, he would just dump her like he had all the others. Old love 'em and leave 'em Jon would strike again and go back on the prowl.

* * * * *

In moments, Jon returned — carrying a coil of rope.

"What's that for?" Darlene asked.

"I thought I'd make sure you have an authentic experience watching *Alice in Bondageland*. So how about I secure your wrists and ankles — give you a chance to feel some of what Alice does while you watch. Is that okay with you?" He held up an end of the rope, bringing it over so Darlene could touch it.

The warm sparks Darlene felt in the pit of her stomach, the tickle in her pussy, signaled exactly how okay it was. On one level. On another level, that of her vampire nature, it would be extremely difficult for her to let a human male restrain her in any way. Her immediate reaction to being tied would be to break free — and destroy whoever and whatever tried to impede her freedom.

But she wanted this experience. She wanted what Jon was offering so much, she had to focus on keeping her vampire strength under wraps—so he'd have the illusion he was dominating her. Because her gut and her heart and her spirit were doing cartwheels in anticipation of his rope trick.

Chapter Four

From Veronica Vampira's Secret Diaries:
How will I know when my true one, my prince among men, has come for me? Will he gallop passionately up to me on the back of his shiny white horse, gleaming in the brilliant moonlight of an inky black midnight sky, the stars glittering and twinkling ecstatically like a perfect band of diamonds against a background of the finest exotic ebony silk?

Lynette got into Nick's shiny new SUV. Black. Nice car. The import-export business must be good…

"That's a big car, especially for San Francisco."

Nick shrugged. "I use it to cart things around for my business, so it's practical. Even here."

Nick lived in a cottage a short distance from Happy Humping. He parked in the driveway behind the larger house closer to the street. Then he came around to open the door for Lynette. He put his hand on her back to guide her to his place, tucked behind the house, out of sight of the street.

The blue cottage, with its sloped roof, its two windows sporting boxes of plants, and its pretty white door looked like something out of the fairy tales Lynette had read when she was a kid. Cottages always seemed so much more *romantic* than the garden apartments her family lived in when she was growing up. Funny how, over the years, she lost all those early notions of what was romantic. Not lost, but maybe hid from Darlene—and herself. Maybe now was the time to let the romance in her soul breathe again. Darlene would never know.

"It's small, but it's home." Nick opened the door to the living room. Lynette's immediate impression was of a rush of jewel colors—sapphire, emerald, ruby, and topaz with lots of wood and plants.

Nick had two loveseats, covered in a blue and white stripe, decorated with pillows in primary colors. A white Berber weave rug covered a good section of the gleaming wood floor. Between the two loveseats, a glass coffee table was covered with art books and a white marble sculpture that screamed, "Expensive". A huge painting in more primary colors dominated the wall over a functioning fireplace.

"Did you decorate this place yourself?" Lynette took it all in and liked what she saw.

"I'm not finished yet."

"Looks finished to me." Lynette spotted a dog-eared book on an end table and picked it up. *Romeo and Juliet.* Her total favorite. "Is this part of the furnishings?" She held it up.

"Hey, why not? It's a love story that takes place in Italy. Where my people are from."

"I'd like to go there some day." Lynette sat down and looked through the pages. Nick had marked the passages she loved most. He sat down next to her, and his breath felt warm on her neck as he read the verses to her.

"Maybe we can go to Verona together some time." Nick smiled and waggled his eyebrows.

As if. But she could pretend for now. "I'd like that."

"Can I get you some more wine?"

"I'm fine."

"You're a cheap date."

"In some ways."

He chuckled dryly. "I'll turn on music and light some candles. What do you like?"

"You choose," she said, her voice sounding low and throaty. Her fangs began to descend again. She ran her tongue over them, trying to get them to go away. For now. Maybe she'd be able to have a tasty snack later... Thoughts like that did little to make her fangs disappear.

Neither did it help to watch Nick. He put on some jazz, heavy on the saxophones. Lynette could feel the music setting a mood.

The ten or so vanilla-scented candles Nick lit cast a glow in the darkened room by the time he put his tush next to hers. She put down the book. He put his arm around Lynette and drew her close. With one hand, he massaged the back of her neck, drawing small circles of heat and light. Her nipples sprang to instant attention, and her sexual hunger began to grow. To say nothing of her other hungers. Nick's warmth, his pulsing aliveness, his musky scent, his gorgeous blood now racing through his body—with an amazing amount of it going straight to his cock.

Lynette stifled a groan. Her senses were jumping into overload, and she'd soon explode from the combination of need and overstimulation. Any moment now she'd begin shrieking like a wild banshee, and maybe fly around the room like the feral bat taking wing in her heart. But Nick's steadiness, in combination with his heady sensuality, kept Lynette connected to the earth.

Nick's lips found hers, and Lynette's last rational thought was to get those damned fangs back where they belonged. His lips tasted salty, felt firm, insistent now, demanding that she open to him. Thank the universe, her fangs fully retracted for a moment, and Lynette was right there, savoring the thrust and dance of Nick's tongue as he explored her. His warm breath, fresh with mint, salty from the beer, mingled with her own vital force.

Nick pulled away from her. "Sorry," he said. "Didn't mean to hurt you." What the hell was he sorry for?

She ascended from her fog. "Get back here. You didn't hurt me."

"Didn't I? When I bit you? Sorry, I got carried away."

She couldn't laugh now. Maybe they'd both be able to laugh later. "Get carried away, man. Bite me. Just bring your mouth back here."

Nick quickly complied, this time plunging far deeper than he had before. Damn, she could feel his heartbeat accelerating, and she knew it was all *for* her and *from* her. And not because she scared him.

Willing her fangs to stay put, Lynette chanced her own journey of discovery into Nick. Nick had a generous mouth. Her tongue lapped at his, taking quick inventory of his teeth. She was dying to take a nibble, but what remained of her good sense stopped her. No way those fangs would stay out of the picture if Lynette let her teeth begin to take possession of Nick.

When she withdrew, Nick took over, his lips pressing in to deepen their kiss. She stroked the delicious back of his neck, feeling the spot where his hair curled onto the nape of his neck and wanting to taste him there. And behind his ears. He groaned. His erection must be jammed against his pants, and Lynette wanted to liberate it. Geez, men these days didn't whip it out nearly as quickly as the guys she went to school with. Lynette was about to tear down Nick's zipper when, still kissing her, Nick began to fondle her breasts. Oh, yes. His long, fine fingers got in under her bra and touched her breasts like he was a sculptor and she the finest marble. He skimmed those fingers over her skin, raising goose bumps of pleasure. She longed to jam his fingers harder into her flesh, but she couldn't bear to end the delicious agony of his fingertips tracing a delicate path across the sensitive skin. Her nipples, beaded hard and tight now, were probably poking holes in her bra.

Lynette shivered with a momentary frisson of horror. Tonight she'd put on saggy white cotton panties and the bra that had pictures of a famous duck saying "Quack." As soon as he got an eyeful, Nick would probably wilt like a head of month-old romaine.

On the other hand, the way he was fondling her breasts, teasing the nipples with those magic fingers as he continued to kiss her, maybe nothing would put him off.

She didn't want to take that chance. She wanted that wild ride. "Uh, Nick."

"Yeah." He pulled his tongue from her mouth. "Too hard? Too soft?"

"Just right, Nick. But, uh, I'm thinking I want to, you know, *get more comfortable*." She gazed at him from under hooded eyes. "You know. Way too many clothes. You, me. Let's get out of them."

He looked at her with something akin to adoration in his eyes. "You want to get naked already?"

"Yeah. Let's race and see who can get out of their clothes the fastest."

"You sure are different, baby. Hell, you're on." He stood up and tugged at his shirt.

Faster than she'd have believed possible for a mortal, he stood blissfully and powerfully naked in front of her. His cock rose a magnificent nine fully packed inches.

"The dildo we got looks puny next to you." Lynette admired him, forgetting her concerns about her own underwear.

"See what an effect you have on me?" he asked huskily, poking his rod in her direction. He took himself in hand for a moment, and Lynette nearly came on the spot. "Feeling lonely over here. You haven't even started taking your clothes off."

Lynette gave him the old mesmerizing glare, and Nick's eyelids fluttered before he went into a vacant-eyed pose. While she tore her clothes off and flung them into a corner, Lynette kept her eyes on the prize. Nick didn't lose an iota of turgidness.

"I'm ready." She blinked three times so he'd snap out of it.

Nick gave her a head-to-toe sweep, his tongue at the corner of his lips and his cock throbbing in appreciation. He swept her up in his arms and raced into his bedroom. Lynette looked around for a moment. But a gorgeous guy was carrying her to his bed in his arms. She'd check out the décor later.

Nick reverently lay Lynette down on top of his bed. "You are so incredibly beautiful. Your skin is like the finest porcelain, your body that of a goddess."

No one'd ever said that to her before. "If I'm a goddess, I command you to get on this bed with me."

Nick lay down on his side and started to reach for Lynette. Much as she desired to feel him fill all the right places, she first had to feast her eyes on his sheer masculine gorgeousness. Lynette wanted to touch him everywhere, from his buff pecs, to his sculpted arms, to his flat, flat belly and his powerful thighs. But most especially, his exquisite cock, large, full, and absolutely primed.

She went for his cock first. Well, his cock *and* his balls. Nick made Lynette think of all those classic statues prudes would cover up with fig leaves. She hefted his balls, giving them a good squeeze. Nick shuddered and groaned. Then Lynette circled his cock with her eager fingers, running them up and down his erection twice. He gasped her name. She had an urgent desire to take his cock into her mouth, but doubted she could get her fangs to stay put now—and she didn't want to blow this blowjob.

Okay, so she'd explore later—when she could work out minor kinks like her fangs and, oh yeah, her screaming compulsion to bite deep into her lover and suck his blood. Nick pulled her to him, crushing her breasts against his chest, jamming his cock up against her belly. A warmth she usually experienced only after a great feed crept along Lynette's spine, and all she wanted in the universe was to get closer, closer, ever closer to Nick. Now their legs entwined, seemingly of their own volition.

Nick was running his hands up and down her back, kissing her hotly and deeply. To her happy surprise, Lynette began to lose herself in the sensation of being with him—to relax, confident that her fangs would stay put 'til she wanted them. For this moment, the woman in her took precedence over the vampire.

Nick was amazingly strong, his hands sure wherever he touched. Lynette fingered his small hard nipples, reveling in their responsiveness to the slightest contact. It was too delicious having his tongue in her mouth for her to break the kiss and lick those tempting nipples. Later. She'd come back to those nipples later.

"I want to lick you everywhere," Nick said when he withdrew from their kiss. He touched her lips with his fingers, whispering huskily in her ear. "You have such an amazing body."

"Mmm," she murmured, running her foot up his leg. "Sounds delicious."

"I want to lick you like an ice-cream cone on a hot summer day."

"You think I'm going to melt if you don't lick fast enough?"

"Are you?"

She squeezed his cock. "I'm going to self-destruct if I don't get you in me soon."

He licked the side of her face as he reached down to touch her moist pussy. "Mmm," he said, "I love the way you feel." With infinite slowness, he stroked Lynette's folds, and she pushed her pussy harder against his hand. She wanted to feel him everywhere. There. And there. And there.

"Yeah, baby." He inserted one finger, then a second. Lynette began to ride his fingers, and her moistness became a small torrent. She ran her fingernails the length of his cock, and he inhaled sharply. "I just need to reach over for a condom," he said in a choked voice.

Lynette was about to tell him that it *definitely* wasn't necessary, but decided it was too much information for her to give him just now.

She watched as he rolled the ridged latex over his cock.

Finished, he kissed her pussy, running his tongue up her slit. Lynette twitched in her need for more of him.

Nick rolled Lynette on her back, then stretched out on top of her. He opened her legs with his knee, and kissed her as his cock made contact with her waiting slit.

Lynette groaned the moment Nick entered her. His cock played havoc with her senses as he began to fill her hungry, hungry pussy. With her heightened sensitivity at full alert, Lynette felt each minute twitch and slide of his cock as he moved into her. All her awakened nerve endings reached out to rub against him and luxuriate as he stretched her long unused passage to accommodate his heft and length.

He gasped, no doubt feeling like a thousand little hands were massaging his advancing cock. Moving with the most delicious slowness, Nick overfilled Lynette with a sensuousness she wanted to reach out and make hers forever. A fantasy took over her mind—she was now in a posh Parisian brothel, servicing the heir to the kingdom who would defy all obstacles and make her his queen.

Nick buried his face amazingly near to Lynette's jugular, and she shivered delectably, imagining their roles reversed. What if he were indeed the vampire who was about to initiate her into the mysteries of immortality? But he had no fangs to pierce her—just his tongue and his human teeth which he used to nibble and lick her as he thrust himself deep.

Lynette arched her hips to meet him, falling quickly into the rhythm he set. She clutched his butt, both to hold him tighter and to enjoy the feel of his astounding anatomy.

Nick was, as advertised, a noisy lover, making lots of little sounds to express his surprise and pleasure at how good it was for the two of them. It turned Lynette on even more. Most vampires were extremely silent lovers. When she heard Nick, Lynette remembered how much she'd enjoyed this aspect of lovemaking in the past.

"Lynette, is there something special you want me to do?" Nick lifted his head and gasped. "Somewhere you want me to touch that I'm not getting?"

In response, Lynette clutched his ass tighter and moaned softly. Her fangs were now fully out, and she had to keep her mouth firmly closed. Thank God he wasn't trying to kiss her. It was a losing battle with the fangs. The first time they made it together wasn't supposed to be this good. Lynette was hard-pressed to imagine how lovemaking could be any better than what was happening between the two of them now. She wouldn't even let worry about her fangs cast a cloud over what was happening. For now, she felt there was nothing about her that she wouldn't share with Nick. Just not at this precise moment, when she wanted him to keep all his focus exactly where he had it. On her clit and her core.

Nick was circling with his ass and cock now, doing a new dance—hitting the few places he hadn't touched before. Lynette's clit pulsed with stimulation, shooting pleasure bursts all up and down her body. With a slight gasp, she recognized the beginnings of her first orgasm—light-years better than what she'd managed to produce the night before at that sex club. Determined to keep her mouth shut over her fangs, Lynette began to shudder and shake with the intensity of her relief and her release. Nick, gazing down at her, slowed his thrusts, encouraging her to give full vent to her climax.

Lynette had to clamp her lips down not to scream. She'd never screamed before. But she'd never been so completely caught up in an orgasm. Now she understood about the earth moving. With Nick, everything moved. Earth, moon, stars, some planets out in another galaxy...

"That was luscious," Nick murmured when Lynette subsided. She closed her eyes.

"You're so quiet," he added, stroking her face tenderly with his hand.

She merely nodded. Soon, he'd know why. But she wanted him to come first. Exerting all her willpower, she let her eyes do her talking. And her hands. And her pussy. She arched up to resume their rhythm, and Nick took the hint. "You're ready to start up again?"

She nodded. Difficult as it was to believe, Nick now seemed even harder and bigger than earlier. Lynette never came more than once, so she'd focus on bringing Nick to his climax—and enjoy it. Her fangs didn't retract even now, which was strange. But she couldn't worry about that. Nick was starting to move faster and breathe harder. She thrust up to meet him, grinding her pussy against his cock in a true screwing motion. Too good.

To her amazement, Lynette felt the stirrings of an unprecedented second come. She began to shake with the power of her second arousal, and she found herself in uncharted territory.

Nick raised his head and practically howled. "Lynette!" He screamed out her name—and began to spurt deep into her.

Lynette was right there with him, one moment behind, shaking with a second orgasm that had her teeth rattling, her mouth open, and her fangs way out.

A momentary shock registered in Nick's eyes as he took in the sight of Lynette's mouth wide open and ravenous—and then she rolled him on his side and plunged her fangs deep into his neck.

Nick continued groaning orgasmically as she drank from him, if anything turning her on even more. The glorious, beautiful blood of a healthy young man—warm, brimming with all his energy and life force. And a bonus. Nick was a very special flavor. After a moment's reflection, Lynette realized she was drinking AB negative, the rarest type. Never went on sale at any blood bank. Nicholas LaStrada was a unique man in more ways than one.

With her aroused appetite, Lynette had to be careful not to drink too much from him. Of course she would never drink enough to kill or permanently harm him, but if she wasn't careful she could seriously deplete his vital energy. And she definitely did not want that to happen tonight. So after her first delectable drink, she reluctantly withdrew and gently licked Nick's puncture wounds to heal them.

* * * * *

Nick didn't know what hit him. He'd had sex with many women before, even made love with a good number of them. But nobody ever hit all his senses—affected him on the cellular level — like Lynette. He connected with her in so many ways, it was almost scary.

When he rode her, her pussy surrounded him with liquid silk and velvet, a sensation unlike any he'd ever experienced. And when Lynette took him into her, it was beyond a joining of two bodies. Like she was sucking him into her, and they'd be forever joined.

He felt her everywhere. With her mouth on his neck, the top of his head came to life and he felt himself grow. His toes tingled with energy, forcing his awareness there too. And his cock once again grew hard, though he'd just spurted his cum. Every part of him grew and hummed while Lynette nestled under his chin.

With her there, he could almost imagine confiding in her the deepest, darkest of his desires. Beyond the impulse to have a woman fuck him up the ass with a dildo, he wished one day to find himself in the arms of a vampire. The creature of his most secret dreams and desires.

But he didn't want to press his luck. Enough that Lynette agreed to fuck him with the dildo. More than enough that the lovemaking with her blew his mind. Deep as he regarded the communication between them, he couldn't risk telling her the rest. Could he?

He'd continue to rely on his instincts. So far, they'd worked out beautifully, leading him to this moment with Lynette.

* * * * *

Lynette hovered above Nick to gauge his reaction. He appeared the slightest bit paler than before — hardly noticeable with his olive complexion. But he also seemed dazed. No real surprise there. Lynette knew Nick wasn't real clear on what had just happened to him. If she wanted to, she could easily extend his state of ignorance. With just a flick of her eyelids, she could wipe out his memory of the past few minutes, and they'd just continue on with the evening's fun and games.

Lynette was feeling the power of her special attributes. She had total control of what was going to happen for Nick. She could come out to him as a vampire, or she could go back to hiding her identity, which had worked fine all night. Hell, she could probably come up with a formula to keep concealing her fangs from him — even when they were in full sight.

Not. The moment she thought about wiping away his memories, a big black claw clutched at her heart and stopped her, as much as anything in heaven or earth could.

Lynette smacked up against a brick wall — her inner voice. She had to admit to herself that she really didn't want to erase her first feeding from him. Because something about what just happened between her and Nick was too big to ignore. She wanted something real with him — more than a dishonest roll in the hay.

Hell, what did she have to lose by coming clean?

Everything. He might go running out into the night, maybe straight to some insane asylum he'd view as a refuge. Or maybe he'd call the cops, ask for the special vampire hunters' lieutenant. Or, maybe, just maybe, he'd be ready to take their relationship to a whole new level.

Nick was groaning louder now and beginning to stir. His eyelids blinked rapidly as if he was trying to assimilate some weird and shocking sight. In just a moment, he'd start asking questions. He began to move.

Lynette could just make a joke that, in the throes of passion, she'd bitten him harder than she'd intended. As she watched him, a new, captivating warmth took hold of her. Lynette thought back to their conversation, to Nick confiding his most secret desires to her. He'd taken a chance exposing himself to her like that, a stranger he'd just met. He'd put his feelings on the line, his needs and vulnerabilities—and started burrowing into her heart.

Could she do less for him?

"Man, I've never come like that before." He pronounced his words slowly and carefully, like a drunk trying to explain himself. "But at the end, it felt like…"

"What did it feel like, Nick?" Lynette asked.

He shook his head. "Like sharpness and powerful sucking." He looked at her wonderingly. "Lynette, what the hell did you do to me?" His eyes hooded, he rubbed the side of his neck where she'd fed.

Crunch time. "Nick, I've got something really major to tell you."

He stopped rubbing his neck and looked at her, warily.

"I'm listening." He focused completely on her.

"You were so honest with me before, when you told me about your fantasy of being fucked by a woman."

"Yeah." He studied her for a moment, thinking. "Lynette, are you gonna tell me about some sort of fetish, something maybe a little kinky…?"

"Not exactly, Nick. It goes deeper than that. You with me?"

"Are you kidding? You've got my full attention. I just want to tell you, you don't have to worry about what you say. Because what I confided in you was only one of my fantasies. I still haven't told you my greatest fantasy."

"You haven't?" That rattled Lynette. What other secrets lurked in Nick's heart? Or was he just saying that to encourage her to relax?

"No. I want to hear yours first. And, *God*, the way you're lying here with me, all beautiful and sexy. In another minute or so, you're going to have my full erection, er...*attention*, again. If you want it. I've never been this turned on before in my life. You can tell me whatever you want."

"I'm a vampire."

She said the words so quickly, they flew incomprehensibly by him. She repeated the words a bit slower. "Nick, I'm...a...vampire."

He looked at her with disbelief starting to register on his face. Then he laughed. "Is this one of those Goth games or something? You've taken on the persona of a vampire?" He rubbed his neck once more. "Very well, I might add."

"No game, Nick. No games between us unless we both agree to them. I'm a vampire."

He blinked his eyes rapidly and took a deep breath. "Are you telling me you're a real, honest-to-god bloodsucking creature of the night?"

"That's one way I've heard us described. These days, we get most of our food from the local blood bank. Put it on our charge card, free delivery for Internet orders over one hundred dollars."

He shook his head. "That's hard to believe. I mean the vampire part, not the free delivery."

"I imagine so. How can I convince you?"

He thought for a moment. "Can you turn into a bat?"

She wrinkled her nose. "Haven't done it in a while. I'm a bit rusty, but if that's what it takes… I'd be depositing bat pellets all over your clean furniture and floors as I fly over, you know."

"No thanks. Okay, Lynette, okay. So you think you're a vampire. So show me your fangs."

"Done." She opened her mouth. Her fangs had still not retracted, so Nick got instant gratification.

Nick gulped twice at the view of her gleaming canines. "That hallucination I had that you were sucking my blood…"

"That was no delusion, man. You're type AB negative, and you are a scrumptious feast."

Now he looked at her with dawning acceptance. "Lynette, you won't believe this. You're my biggest fantasy come true! I've always wanted to be with a beautiful vampire. No wonder making love with you has been the most mind-blowing experience of my life! You have it all. *And* you said you're going to fuck me with the dildo. Geez, this is the most amazing night of my life."

And the most amazing *since* her life. Lynette felt a sneaky warmth in the region of her heart as something unique started to take shape in the way she looked at, and felt about Nick. She could almost see Darlene, smirking somewhere in the background and gushing about romance and love and all that. Much as she cared for her friend, Lynette pushed her image off into the mist.

Maybe getting into some hot and heavy sex would distract her wandering thoughts from going into unwelcome territory. "So where did you say that dildo was?" she asked, her voice coming out wobbly.

"You mean you're still willing to do me with a dildo?"

"Hey, it's part of our deal tonight. First we made amazing love, regular man- woman style."

"Yeah, but we didn't talk about the vampire games," he pointed out.

"A bonus," she said. "Go get the dildo. And the harness. I feel like I've been waiting far too long to try this out."

"You're amazing." Nick kissed her lingeringly. Fully erect now, he broke away and went over to the table where they'd left the new goodies. With a huge grin on his face, Nick handed them over.

Lynette shivered deliciously as she ran her hands over the dildo and harness. Despite her recent orgasms, her clit twitched at the heft and feel of the dildo. They'd picked very well.

"Have you ever done it with anyone using this?"

Nick pursed his lips. "You're my first in this, too."

Lynette chuckled. "We're both dildo virgins."

"Not for long."

"So how do we, uh, get set up here?" She held both the harness and the dildo up. Her pussy lips pumped moisture as she got ready for action. She wasn't sure how much physical satisfaction she'd get from her role, but she wanted to do this for Nick. And *with* him. She wanted to fulfill this long-held fantasy, to be the first woman ever to be with him like this.

Only thing was, it looked complicated.

"First off, I understand it's best to put a condom on the dildo and lubricate it. So things go smoothly."

"Okay. What kind of lubricant do you have?"

"Several hundred kinds. But I think for this particular position, we'll just go with the plain, ordinary, garden-variety lubricant in a tube."

Lynette held the dildo as Nick unfurled a condom on it. His hand brushed hers, and she once again noticed how right his touch felt to her. Comforting and exciting, all in one. She liked being able to see the contours of the dildo through the condom.

Once they had the dildo good to go, the condom gleaming with lubricant, they turned their attention to the harness. "Do I put this on first and then fit the dildo in, or attach the dildo and then put the harness on?"

"According to the directions," Nick said, looking up from a small card, "the second choice. We put it all together and then strap it on you."

"So you're one of those people who reads the fucking manual, huh?"

"Guilty as charged."

They managed to get the dildo strapped on Lynette without too many false starts. When she was in harness, so to speak, Lynette looked down at the erect penis jutting from her body. She'd never before imagined being in this position, and now she found she enjoyed it. A new surge of power, quite unlike her vampire strength, coursed through her veins.

If she had any regrets, it was maybe that they hadn't gotten a double-headed one. She wanted to join in on the fun, to have the friction of a hard cock stimulating her pussy as they played. Maybe next time, if there ever was one...

And then they were ready to go. First Nick took her in his arms, wanting to kiss her. They both laughed as his cock and hers collided. Then he rubbed his cock against hers as he probed deep into her mouth with his tongue, nibbling on her lips. They broke apart.

Wordlessly, he put his hands on the wall and bent from his waist. His gorgeous butt gleamed temptingly before her. Lynette was about to enter him when she remembered the lubricant. She stroked his skin, then bent over and licked his ass, her tongue darting in and out of his hole. Nick groaned, and a shiver went up her spine at how strongly she was affecting him.

Lynette positioned her new cock at the edge of Nick's now well-lubricated hole and began to thrust. She quickly slid down his crack, which was not the desired trajectory. Nick pushed closer to Lynette, and she picked up the dildo and tried again to enter him. No luck. This was harder than she'd thought it would be.

"Maybe put your hands on my hips for leverage," Nick said, sounding hoarse. After all, he was close to living out his fantasy. She didn't want to screw things up now.

Leaning over more than she'd expected to, Lynette was able to clutch Nick's hips. But then she had to move one of her hands down to the dildo again to steer it. So with one hand on Nick and one on the dildo, she finally hit pay dirt. She could feel Nick's muscles relaxing, letting her in. Or rather, the dildo. She wanted to let out a whoop of joy.

Nick gasped when she finally entered him fully. And then he began to move, and she fell into the rhythm he started, moving the length of the dildo in and out of his ass with the thrust of her hips. She could almost feel the pleasure he did, like an echo reverberating in her deepest core. One of them moaned, or maybe it was both.

Nick now had just one hand on the wall, the other on his cock. As Lynette arched in and out of him, he stroked his massive erection, his hand keeping the rhythm the two of them had established in back. Lynette could watch as he touched his own flesh, which turned her on as much as everything else they were doing. When Nick grew large and his accelerated breathing told her he was about to come, Lynette picked up the pace, moving back and forth like a smoothly running piston. She was so caught up in their mutual motion that she screamed with surprise and release when Nick began to come and come and come.

And then it was over. He turned around, pulling her to him in an embrace of gratitude, and relief, and far more. He kissed her, then unstrapped the harness and threw it aside.

"Your turn," he said, laying Lynette down on the bed. He gently parted her legs, and buried his face in her hungry pussy. Lynette, who'd never been this aroused before, grabbed a handful of Nick's hair, willing herself not to hurt him. And she wound her legs around his neck to give him the best access to her waiting folds.

Nick lapped at her hungrily, tonguing every last inch of her pussy, her swollen clit. "Yes, oh yes," Lynette moaned, as his tongue and teeth performed magic. She moved against his mouth and teeth with all the need that had built up over her long, fallow time. Though she knew it was far too soon for him to get hard again, she wanted to be penetrated as well as eaten. He slurped at her with big sloppy kisses and licks, jamming one finger, then two into her. She swung her hips like a wild woman, in a frenzied search for that elusive climax.

"I'll be right back," he whispered. He left her for a moment, and Lynette grabbed at her pussy, rubbing, tossing her head from side to side. Nick returned, brandishing the dildo. "Fresh condom and lubricant," he said, "though you hardly need the latter." His mouth glittered with her juices. Nick began to kiss her again as he quickly guided the dildo where she wanted it.

Flailing madly, she thrust her hips against the dildo while Nick managed to hold on, licking her, biting her, touching her everywhere. Lynette almost didn't want to give in to her climax, the sensations were so overwhelming. But she couldn't hold back. In moments, Lynette was coming, her howls of delight and release reaching far into space.

And then, with difficulty, she subsided. Nick was petting her the whole time. When she'd calmed to little shivers and whimpers of delight, he lay down next to her and held her in his arms.

Lynette couldn't find words to express what she'd just experienced. Nick recovered his tongue first. "I wish you could stay here. We've only begun to get to know each other."

"Yes."

"I want to be with you again. Tomorrow night?"

"Yes, oh yes. But tomorrow, at my house."

"Whatever you wish, my darling one. Always."

They lay together 'til he absolutely had to get her home before her strict curfew.

Chapter Five

From Veronica Vampira's Secret Diaries:
My heaving heart is in bottomless bondage, twisting and
turning restlessly in my never-ending journey in search of the
ultimate perfection of the languid lips of the one I will one day
and forever adore…

When Darlene hadn't said anything for several moments, Jon put down the coil of rope. "It's fine for you to think carefully before you agree to anything."

"I want us to go ahead with whatever you have planned." Darlene waved her hand nonchalantly and hoped she hadn't inadvertently done something to scare him off.

"Thank you for that permission." He looked at her warily. "You know, Darlene, I think we can be important to each other. I don't want to do anything that will threaten what's happening between us."

Her heart clenched when he said the words. "You're not."

"Good. But still, judging from the expression on your face, you seem to have a problem deciding. What can I say to make your decision easier? More than anything else, I want your trust," he said, his voice gentle.

She shook her head, amazed at how much insight into her he seemed to have. "Sorry, Jon. There's no question about my trusting you, because I do." He couldn't hurt her physically. Emotionally yes. But she was only here for one night's adventure, right? "My concerns have to do with me, not you."

He backed away. "Do what's right for you. Always. Look, if you want, we can just watch the video without doing anything else. I don't even have to tie you up."

"Thank you." She knew she could opt out, but she needed to rise to the dare he'd brought up. She nodded and smiled. "I want you to tie me up. I want to feel like Alice while I watch. It'll be far more educational." She steeled her resolve.

He exhaled. "Now you look and sound sure, Darlene. I'm glad. But before we start, I want you to know this. You can stop whatever happens between us any time you want, for any reason. Do you know what a safe word is?"

"Not exactly."

"A safe word is one we agree on, beforehand. Any time you want things to stop, all you have to do is say that word."

"What should it be?"

"You decide and tell me. Some word you wouldn't say to me for any reason other than you me to stop what I'm doing."

Darlene's mind raced over all the possibilities, and she instantly knew the perfect name to stop all action. "Editor."

"Editor?" he repeated.

She nodded, pleased.

"Okay. Any time you say the word *editor*, I'll stop what I'm doing. Now hold out your hands." Swallowing her last hesitation, she clasped her hands in front of her and held them up high. When he wrapped the first coil around her wrists, she nearly punched him out. Only with great effort could she swallow back her defensive action and leave herself open to him. She didn't know how long she'd be able to hold back.

"You have such beautiful hands." Jon pulled the circle of rope tight enough to make things uncomfortable, yet not tight enough to cut off the circulation. In the welter of her emotions, Darlene recognized that Jon knew what he was doing.

With her wrists bound snugly, Jon turned to Darlene's ankles. "Slip off your shoes."

A wave of self-consciousness about her ugly feet washed over Darlene as she kicked off her black flats and waited for him to send her away in disgust.

When he said nothing, Darlene began to relax. He proceeded to massage her feet, still encased in nylon knee-highs, and made them feel wonderful. Once she got over her initial fears, she wondered if he'd ask her to take off the footwear also, then realized that would be a problem with her hands bound. But he didn't. "Great feet. How come no polish on those gorgeous toenails?" He ran his fingers over them, pinching her toes several times — which excited Darlene far out of measure with his casual attitude. "Pedicures are so much fun…"

"I'll have to get one." A pedicure jumped to the head of her to-do list.

"Maybe sometime I can give you one."

"Sounds like heaven."

"And maybe sometime we can talk about where to shop for some really amazing clothes. Corsets and the like."

Darlene cringed, remembering Lynette's disdainful comments.

Letting him bind her ankles didn't challenge Darlene nearly as much as the tying of her wrists. Maybe Darlene had harnessed her defensive reflex. She savored the feeling of the rope pulled so tightly around her ankles that her pussy folds pressed tight over her clit—raising the level of her arousal.

Jon sat down very close to her and put his arms around her. "Now we're ready to watch the video."

Darlene snuggled into Jon as the images began to flash across the scene. He held her, his arm around her shoulders. Sometimes he would pull her very tightly, almost painfully, to him. Darlene wondered if she was supposed to protest, but decided she enjoyed the clinch far too much to put him off with a complaint.

Darlene's first surprise as the video began was the excellence of the sound and picture quality.

The scene opened with a longhaired young blonde— obviously Alice—running through a field in what looked like England. Though a gorgeous young nobleman was running after her, calling her name, she persisted in her flight. He'd nearly caught her when she fell down a very large rabbit hole and landed smack in the middle of a tea party.

"There you are," a large naked woman wearing a huge crown trilled when Alice landed in a chair with a teacup and plate before her. "Do you want crumpets or scones with your tea? Clotted cream or raspberry jam?"

"Just tea, thank you," Alice said in a little girl voice, surprising in someone with such huge naked breasts.

"You're late," said a man who looked like a rabbit and had an amazingly long erect cock. He pointed to a huge pocket watch with thick fingers.

Alice furrowed her brow. "I'm so sorry. But you see, I had no idea we had an appointment today."

"You forgot our appointment? You know what that means." The man smirked to Alice and his companions. He put the watch back in his pocket.

"No, I don't know what that means. Please tell me."

"When people forget their appointments, they must be punished." His eyes gleamed. Then his face grew harsh. "Well, what are you waiting for, young Alice? Get up. It's way past time to go."

Alice rose to her full height. The rabbit-man stared directly at her stiff nipples, which were slightly below his eye level, and his erect penis began to twitch. "Way past time to go," he echoed, smacking her on the ass.

"Ow," she complained, her eyes filling with tears. She looked at the crowned woman for help, but she had already disappeared.

Alice followed the man. Darlene watched Alice as Jon continued to hold her and watch her. To her surprise, he tightened the ropes again. She hadn't imagined they could be much tighter.

The idea that Alice was being punished fascinated Darlene. Her spine tingled deliciously, and she toyed with the idea of asking Jon all about what punishment signified here. But maybe she should continue watching and figure things out for herself.

The rabbit-man fastened a studded dog collar around Alice's neck and tied a rope around her waist. He led her to his home, practically at a run. Rabbit-man's house turned out to bear a strong resemblance to Darlene's own lair. Her heart sped up at this. Could Jon possibly know where she and Lynette lived — was that why he chose this video to show Darlene?

When Alice got inside his house, the man took her over his knee, arranged her carefully over his erection, and spanked her butt red with a huge wooden paddle. While Alice sobbed out loud each time a blow landed, Darlene could also see her manipulating herself around the man's penis. Alice's face was a mixture of pain and sexual arousal. Darlene's nipples grew stiff with longing as she watched. Though tight in Jon's embrace, she began to squirm.

Jon abruptly stopped the video. "What are you thinking?"

"Thinking?" Darlene answered, not believing anything that was going on in her head right now qualified as thinking.

Jon dug his fingers harshly into Darlene's shoulder, surprising her — thrilling her. "I'd appreciate an answer to my question," he said calmly.

"I did answer you," she said, "with a question."

He pinched her again, hard. "That doesn't count. I want to know what's going on in that pretty head of yours, what's making you squirm in the seat. And your role here is to do what I tell you." He looked dead serious as he said this.

Darlene knew what a joke it was for him to think he had any control over her, but evidently he thought he did. She could end that real quickly, but that wouldn't be playing the game they seemed to have embarked on. And she had gotten involved in tonight's adventure to learn.

It was all a game, she reminded herself. Just for tonight, she was Darlene, a woman who let herself be picked up at Happy Humping. So she was acting, something she wasn't all that good at. She found it so hard to pretend that she toyed with saying the safe word. Editor. An image of Edna Edmore and her rejection letter ran through Darlene's mind. But tonight was all about experiencing new things in order to expand Veronica's repertoire. Not to mention that Darlene was dying of curiosity and sexual arousal. Okay, not exactly dying. But panting after.

No, even though she was getting a bit weirded out by the things Jon was doing, she was more turned on than she could remember ever being before... She'd take the next step with Jon, wherever that took her.

"I'm squirming because I'm incredibly turned on," she said, her voice sounding strange to her. "My panties are so wet with desire, I could nearly wring them out."

"A good start."

Jon's fingers traced a line of fire down between her breasts, extending to her pussy. It felt amazingly sensuous the first time, but then he pressed harder, which Darlene didn't like nearly as much. Just as she was about to protest, he kissed her—a kiss she felt down to her toes. "Are you ready to watch more of the video?" His hot breath fanned her ear.

"Yes." She wanted to start making some sense of what was going on.

Jon rewound the tape a bit. They again watched Alice squirming on the man's lap as he smacked her bottom. Darlene wondered what Jon's cock would feel like pressed against her. Was he getting aroused by the video or by her? When would she find out what effect she had on him?

The rabbit-man ordered Alice to get on her hands and knees on his bed. She meekly agreed.

Rabbit-man now stood between the camera and Alice and, smirking, held up what looked like metal cuffs and chains. "I'm going to put these on you now."

"Thank you." She looked grateful. None too gently, he put the cuffs on Alice and, making sure with yet another swat to her rear that she stayed on her hands and knees, attached her arms and legs to the bed posts. Darlene—knowing she'd have to really subdue her vampire strength to permit herself to be chained like that—tingled at the prospect.

The rabbit-man blindfolded Alice. Darlene nearly snorted. With her vampire vision, she'd be able to see through any blindfold. To her surprise, she envied Alice her ability to really be in the dark. But she wondered how Alice felt. Had she and the rabbit-man come up with a safe word? Darlene didn't remember seeing that. She asked Jon. "Watch the video," he snapped. "I want you to see everything that happens."

Darlene supposed his harsh tone was part of the game and not a real indication that Jon was annoyed, but she inwardly cringed at this kind of rejection. She pushed that thought away as she watched the action.

Rabbit-man was now large and fully erect. He must have had ten inches of hard cock jutting out in front of him. Darlene made a mental note to remember him for a Veronica story.

He ran his cock across Alice's still red cheeks. She began to shake, the nipples of her full breasts erect. Alice, evidently trying to move the only part of herself she could, rolled her head around. As she still wore the dog collar, she resembled a collie. The man grabbed a handful of hair and pulled her head up. "Stay still unless I tell you to move," he barked.

Alice whimpered.

He tied a length of what looked like black silk around her mouth. No way would a gag work on a vampire. If Jon had anything like that in mind for her, she'd have to use her safe word. The alternative was too scary to think about.

Now rabbit-man went behind Alice and lifted her ass up so the camera got a clear shot of the moist pink lips of her mound. Then, without saying another word, he jammed his cock deep inside her. Darlene flinched, almost involuntarily contracting her pussy muscles to deal with the strange pleasure that watching the rabbit-man inside Alice produced.

Rabbit-man began to hump Alice back and forth with long, hard strokes. He had his hand on her ass, emphasizing the up and down of their movements in tandem.

Rabbit-man's rhythm accelerated. He was intensely focused on fucking Alice. That was the only word for it, his cock fucking in and out faster and faster as his large balls banged back and forth. And then he pulled his cock out of Alice and began to spurt cum, a huge white stream that he rubbed into Alice's ass.

The video ended before Darlene was ready. She wanted to see the man free Alice, so she could know what was going to happen next. Was there any affection between the two of them after their intercourse? Though

Darlene wanted to ask Jon, she'd learned enough already not to. Maybe later, when she was no longer bound hand and foot, she'd ask.

"So what did you think of the video?" Jon asked, his eyes narrowed.

"Quite interesting."

"Interesting? Okay, Darlene." He ran his fingers tantalizingly over her mound, and Darlene's pussy spasmed. "You know the saying about art imitating life?"

"Yes."

"Well tonight, I want life to imitate art." He held up some cuffs that looked like the ones from the video. "Let's go to my bedroom now so we can try these out." To punctuate his words, he ran his hand over her pussy slit. Darlene closed her eyes, sure he could feel her moistness through her panties. At the touch of his hand on her clit, she nearly jumped off the loveseat and broke her bindings.

"I think you want what I want," he added, his eyes glittering.

"Uh, one problem. How am I going to get to your bedroom with my feet bound?"

"Hop."

Darlene knew she could have said "Editor", but she wasn't going to. She hopped off the loveseat, held her bound hands out in front of her, and said, "Lead on."

Darlene hadn't noticed before how perfect Jon's bed was for a duplication of the scene she just watched on video. Even though it was a king-size, the bars at the head and foot would accommodate bondage quite handily. "Are you going to do everything the same as we saw in the video?" she asked, most concerned about the effect being gagged would have on her.

Jon looked at her sternly. "I don't believe you had permission to ask a question." Darlene couldn't help noticing the prominent bulge in his pants. Though he was acting cool and in super control, Darlene knew all that was happening was exciting him. It excited her, too.

He commanded her to sit down on the bed, then freed her hands and feet at last. Of course, the ropes had little effect on Darlene the vampire. But she knew Darlene the woman would have some reaction to being freed. So she circled her hands and feet, as if to restore the circulation.

Jon let her do that for about two seconds before he commanded, "Enough. Take off your clothes." He picked up a flogger and Darlene shivered. The rabbit-man had spanked Alice's bare bottom, with a paddle, not a whip of any kind…

Did he mean a striptease or just the kind of disrobing she did every morning before she changed into her pajamas and climbed into her coffin?

"I'm waiting." He impatiently flicked the flogger. It made a sharp whistling sound as it sliced through the air.

Darlene winced involuntarily. But the spirit of Veronica and the challenge of topping Lynette spurred Darlene on. Not to mention the Comte's mission. Wanting to rattle Jon just a bit, she undressed with lightning speed. He blinked to see her standing stark naked in front of him.

Darlene hadn't been stark naked in front of anyone or anything in a very long time. She'd never been an especially exhibitionistic type, and her normal first instinct would be to cover up her breasts and pussy. But, despite the softness and imperfections of her body now, she dared herself to stand straight and proud before Jon's scrutiny.

"You're very pale. Like you never get any sun."

"An allergy."

"Whatever. I like your whiteness. Hell, some people use powder or other makeup, and they don't manage to look nearly as good as you do. Natural."

Darlene stifled her chuckle at that, looked at him and saw his pants bulge out more than before. Evidently her lack of color and everything else about her body were having the desired effect.

"Stand perfectly still," he barked, coming closer. He put the flogger down carefully on an end table and ran his hands over her body, raising goose bumps wherever he touched her with his callused fingers.

"Good," he said at last. "Now I'm going to sit down in the chair across from the bed. Lie across my lap, just the way you saw Alice do."

Did that include squirming to maximize contact with the man's erection? Darlene wondered as she draped herself over Jon and made contact with his very impressive cock.

Jon positioned himself in an ebony wood chair, his legs spread out in a vee from his crotch, his erection tenting up his pants in the most beguiling way. Darlene, whose pussy now ached for attention, lay down over his lap. His cock hit her tantalizingly at her navel, which was fun but not nearly enough to meet her growing needs. She wriggled to slide farther down, so her clit would land strategically over his cock and she could treat herself to some targeted thrusting.

But Jon didn't appear ready to indulge her yet. He put his arms around her and, grunting, powerfully pulled her back to her first position.

Darlene really wanted to rub her clit against that gorgeous bulge now. She repeated her previous slide, and he once again put her back where she'd been. Before she had a chance to move or say a word, she felt a stinging on her butt. Once, twice, three times. Her blood supply began to move to her cheeks, which probably looked even redder than Alice's.

Wherever Jon's blows—which now came faster—landed, Darlene experienced a stinging like a swarm of wasps attacking. Pain, but something else. Something much more subtle and exciting. Darlene bit back a moan of pleasure and arousal, as her clit began to throb so strongly, she was sure he must feel it though the leg of his leather pants.

Jon's cock was now jammed more intensely against her belly, and Darlene grew more excited to feel how his level of arousal was rising. She couldn't help herself now. She opened her legs so her clit was fully pressed to his leg, and she began rubbing herself against him like his leg was a tree trunk and her pussy a small furry animal with a mighty itch. The pressure sent shooting stars up and down her spine, and Darlene's fangs began to lower. She didn't know where to focus first, her pussy caught up in a streaming riot of sensation or her fangs.

"Lie still," he commanded, planting his firm hand between the crack of her ass. "I'll let you know when you're ready for what you want."

If only he knew everything she wanted...

He spanked her seven more times, each smack coming stronger and faster than the one before. "Your ass is beginning to glow like a red light," he growled. "But here red light doesn't mean stop. It's like the lights whores put up over their houses in Amsterdam. It means you're good to go, doesn't it?"

Was she supposed to talk now? Her fangs were fully descended, and there was no way she could get them to retract. Not until she had the satisfaction she was dying for—above and below. Her need to feed fast was outstripping her sexual arousal. And, if memory served correctly, she could feed a lot faster than she'd be able to come. Especially because she was only going to drink a small, controlled amount from Jon. She wanted him at full power for when he finally gave her what she wanted.

He spanked her again. "Why didn't you answer me when I asked you a question?" he spat out.

In response, Darlene hoisted herself up and turned to face Jon.

"Wha—?" he started to ask.

She opened her mouth in her vampire smile. The moment he got a clear view of her fangs, Jon's eyes popped open and he dropped the black bristled brush he'd been using on her tush.

"What the hell?"

"I'm hungry now." Darlene greedily eyed his jugular.

He exhaled. "Good trick, but not part of this scene." He started to reach around her.

"It is now," Darlene countered, tired of waiting.

"Hey, Darlene, those fangs almost look real..."

They are real, she thought, as she took her first delicious swallow.

* * * * *

117

Jon hadn't been with anyone as naïve as Darlene in years. At first, he found it refreshing. In spite of her nowhere clothes and hairdo, she had definite potential. Especially with the way she was eyeing the whips. From the start, Jon's gut told him she'd be a natural. In his mind, he knew from the moment they met what the night's script would look like.

And then... Things got away from him. At first, he wondered what planet Darlene came from. Her reactions were too bizarre. But that put an edge on everything, heightened the arousal potential. Darlene had him hot in ways he hadn't been in years.

But that still didn't challenge his control. But now, she'd stepped way out of line. Her head on his neck. The most incredible sucking sensation. Like she was waking up every nerve ending in his body, daring him to be fully alive.

Whatever it was, he wanted more of it. On his terms.

* * * * *

Jon was a luscious type B negative. Tasting his rich, dark blood, Darlene winced, remembering all of Lynette's recent complaints about the monotony of their diet. She admitted to herself that Lynette was right on this one. Variety would be the keyword for their lives from now on.

Darlene mentally smacked herself. She couldn't believe she was thinking about *shopping* as she hungrily lapped up Jon's heady blood brew. She had to be real careful not to overdo, which meant focusing. Just a bit more, and she'd have to stop herself. Though not fully sated, her Jon snack would tide her over for a while.

When she'd taken her last drops, Darlene gently swept her tongue over the marks she'd made in Jon's neck.

Now she'd be able to wait a bit before she finally got the orgasm she so craved.

But first, she had to deal with Jon, who appeared to be in a state of shock. He'd turned quite pale, far more so than the amount of blood she drank justified, and his heart was thumping so loud it sounded like a set of large drums to her sensitive ears.

A smug smile on her face, Darlene backed off and watched Jon, waiting for his first question. She didn't have to wait long.

"You're a vampire?" he asked, his voice filled with awe.

She fluttered her eyelashes flirtatiously. "I am."

"The real deal," he said, still sitting back in his chair. Darlene was gratified to see that he hadn't lost any of his erection during her feed. If anything, his cock seemed to be straining even harder against his fly than before. She licked her lips and inclined her head to him.

"Holy shit!" he exclaimed, jumping to his feet, before rapidly collapsing back into the chair. Darlene could have warned him that any rapid change in height right now would probably make him dizzy—maybe even woozy.

"I've had a fucking *vampire* here all night being my fucking *submissive*. Triple shit! You have no idea what this means to me."

Darlene continued watching him, feeling some amusement and just a bit of detachment. "I guess I don't. Why don't you tell me?"

He bit his lip. "Darlene, you're like what? Ten times more powerful than me? A hundred? You could have beat the shit out of me at any moment. What am I saying? You could *kill* me before I could even scream for help."

She nodded her head back and forth noncommittally. "I suppose I could do those things," she said, "but I generally don't."

"You don't? How the hell do you survive?"

"You've been watching too many horror movies—reading too much pulp fiction. If you want, I can give you a full description. Later. Now we have more important matters to occupy us." She hoped the gaze she fastened on him was seductive rather than scary. Darn, she was so out of practice.

"Matters to occupy us?" he asked, looking wary.

"Oh, yes. For a start, I don't think we got through even half of what I saw happening in the video."

At first he looked as if he didn't understand. Then a light began to glimmer in his eyes. "After the spanking, the rabbit-man bound Alice hand and foot on his bed and proceeded to fuck her."

"Exactly." Darlene's nipples grew hard and her pussy went soft in anticipation of following Alice.

"Uh, I'm going to cuff *you*, attach *you* to my bed. You're not going to cuff me, right? I'm not a submissive."

"So I've gathered. That means I am."

He exhaled loudly. "Just so we understand each other."

"Oh, I think we understand each other."

A ghost of a smile began to hover on Jon's lips. He rose, deliberately this time, and walked over to the cabinet where he kept some of his goodies. He turned to her three times during this quick process, almost as if to assure himself that she wasn't about to jump him. She sat, her legs spread wide so her moist pussy lips were glistening at him.

Jon appeared to gather his confidence—really, arrogance—as the moments went on, and Darlene waited for his next instruction.

"Geez, a vampire here with me," he mumbled under his breath. Then he pointed to the bed. "On your hands and knees, now."

Grinning, Darlene sauntered over to the bed.

"Faster!" Jon barked out, picking up the black bristled brush as if ready to smack her bottom if she didn't comply.

Good. He was hitting his stride again. Darlene got into position, arching her back up so that he got a full view of her butt and pussy. She turned her head quickly, just to make sure Jon's erection was still in full bloom. Large and growing. She turned back around so he wouldn't catch her looking at him.

"Spread those knees wider," Jon commanded. "Like that," he added, putting his hands between her legs and pushing them apart even more.

He walked around the bed and surveyed her from all angles, as if she were a prize sculpture in an expensive gallery. "That'll work."

"Are you sure you're going to be okay with me cuffing and chaining you?" he asked before putting the first cuff on her right hand.

She'd decided to be totally frank with him. "My first reaction is to break out and hurt you," she said, "but I'm not going to do that. I want to submit."

"I can imagine how tough this must be for you," Jon said appreciatively. Darlene preferred it when he barked, but she could sense that he was trying to reach out to her in her full identity with his comment.

"What do you mean?"

He shrugged. "I've read a lot about vampires, their nature. But I never imagined I'd be doing a scene with one."

"Your lucky day. Don't believe everything you read."

"I usually don't," he said. "But this stuff seemed to be from a reliable source. I suppose there's no point blindfolding you."

"I'd see right through whatever you use, but, if you want, you can go through the motions."

"Why not? A little blindfold on my sub turns me on."

"Then let's do it."

"But I suppose the gag wouldn't be a great idea."

Darlene nodded. "Yeah, that might be too much for me to deal with tonight. Maybe if I can overcome my resistance to the cuffs, we can try a gag some other time…" She said the last wistfully, knowing contemporary dating etiquette included never presuming there would be a second meeting.

Jon didn't reply. Instead he slipped the first cuff around Darlene's right wrist, then chained her to the headboard. Chained her quite tight. It would keep her firmly in place if she weren't a vampire. She'd pretend to be as completely imprisoned as the weakest woman. Next Jon attached her on the other side. Then both ankles. Darlene felt like the trussed turkeys she remembered her family roasting for Thanksgiving. She giggled to herself as she wondered where Jon would put the oyster stuffing.

Jon surveyed her again, rubbing his chin in thought. "Lookin' good," he said. So was he. His erection threatened to explode out of his pants.

He held up a length of fine black silk. "Your blindfold, Darlene." He tied it tight, but she could, of course, still see perfectly.

"You remember your safe word."

"I have an excellent memory."

"Of course. And, uh, I guess we don't need a condom."

"Not unless you like using one better than skin to skin."

"Not in this lifetime," Jon said.

He got behind her and smacked her butt twice, hard. Oh, yes, she was ready for him. The spanking only got her more stimulated.

Darlene heard a zipper coming down. She quickly turned to catch a glimpse of his cock. Endowed as fully as rabbit-man but thicker around, she saw with a smile. Then Jon clutched her hips.

Before Darlene knew what hit her, Jon was jammed all the way up her pussy, the full length of his cock buried deep. It felt as magnificent as she'd expected, judging from his bulge. Long, wide, broad. The skin of his shaft rubbed against all her nerve endings, stimulating her everywhere he touched.

She had to remember to play the game, to let him be the one who controlled their movements. Now that he knew she was a vampire, he said her restraints had an added touch of piquancy.

Jon moved the length of his cock in and out of her in wide arcs, pulling out to the very edge before slamming himself back into her. Darlene longed to fall into the same rhythm with him, but held back. That was, after all, the name of the game. He was kneading her cheeks with his strong fingers, at times digging his nails into the tender skin of her butt.

She waggled her tush at him, curious to see what he'd do. Without breaking his stride, he smacked her, hard, then grunted some unintelligible noise. As Jon grew bigger and bigger with his approaching orgasm, he clutched her tighter. He moved faster and faster, no longer withdrawing fully as he pistoned in and out.

When Jon began to come, he screamed out words in a language Darlene had never heard. And then he collapsed on top of her back, his heart beating wildly. Jon tenderly took off her blindfold, then did the same with all the cuffs and told her to sit up.

Darlene still hadn't come. Wordlessly, Jon got a large black and gold vibrator, told Darlene to lie down, and began to stroke her engorged folds quite competently. She'd been so close to the edge, Darlene came quickly. A flicker of disappointment spun through her. She'd wanted to come from the contact with his cock, his fingers, his mouth—anything was preferable to the hunk of black and gold that had accomplished the job.

But her disappointment diminished when Jon took Darlene in his arms and began to cuddle her. She could have stayed exactly like that forever, except she knew dawn had to be coming soon. "That was amazing," Jon said at last. "Everything about tonight has been beyond belief fantastic. But it was only the beginning of what can be so much more."

Jon's extravagant praise surprised and pleased Darlene. Tonight, with him, she'd had a far more amazing adventure than she could have imagined for herself—or Veronica.

"I must see you again," he said.

"Maybe," Darlene replied. "Give me your number. I'll call." She smiled at the neat role reversal of this. He wrote his number on a card and silently handed it to her.

Darlene tossed the card in her bag. "Now I need to go home." And she left.

Chapter Six

From Veronica Vampira's Secret Diaries:
My love will come to me to be my most excellent life-escort,
walking with me hand-in-hand, by my side always, as we
journey joined together jointly through the mysterious mysteries
of the eternal, endless universe, our nights magnificently
crowned with the glittering glory of our immortal love story.

Nick wanted to escort Lynette home, but she insisted on going herself. When he asked how, she just smiled mysteriously and said, "I have my ways."

She certainly did have her ways, he reflected, lying overwhelmed—nearly crushed—by the immensity of the evening. He hadn't drunk nearly enough beer to have hallucinated it all—unless someone had spiked his drinks with a potent drug, more powerful than any he knew about.

A while later, when Nick tried to get out of bed, he couldn't move. Lynette Loring had shown him pleasure beyond anything he ever imagined possible. He smiled exhaustedly at the thought of this woman, a stranger to him a mere day before. Not just a woman. A vampire. A beautiful woman vampire. He thought he was in love.

Though from time to time he'd heard rumors about a whole vampire culture existing *sub rosa* here in San Francisco and in other enclaves around the world, he scoffed at them with his usual skepticism. Tina, a former girlfriend, called him the world's most romantic skeptic, a title he probably deserved. He'd never admitted to her or anyone else his fantasies of making it with a female vampire. He'd always thought there was as much possibility of that as of making it with the Tooth Fairy.

Tonight shook that skepticism, but definitely stirred the romantic part. God, Lynette had everything and was everything he'd ever dreamed of. If he could have designed his perfect woman, she'd have looked, talked, and loved like Lynette. And reacted to him like she did. He adored loud, passionate, generous women—and she'd been all that in her loving.

But, she was a vampire. He ran his hands through his hair. He'd just had the best sex of his life with a freaking vampire—who sucked his blood as part of her climax! He touched his neck where she punctured him with those fangs, which he'd first thought were fake. It didn't take her long to convince him they were real, and so was she.

And even if he'd remained unconvinced about the fangs, he couldn't have held on to his disbelief once she turned into a swirling mist for her trip home.

He ran his hands down his body to assure himself he was not dreaming even now. His butt still ached tantalizingly from the way she'd thrust that dildo up his ass. Nick closed his eyes reliving that, and his penis briefly stirred.

"Down boy," he said. Now that he had Lynette in his life, he had better things to do with erections than whack off. Besides which, he was really wiped.

He was going to be with Lynette again, if she'd have him. How could he resist her? And then he began to wonder. What did it mean to be with a vampire for more than a one-night stand? Of course, they wouldn't have any daytime dates. He could be cool with that.

But there was way more to find out about. Would she fuck him up the butt again? Maybe they should have gotten a double-headed dildo, as the one-way action couldn't have been much fun for her. Not that she'd complained. And he sucked her and played with her to orgasm after, so that seemed okay.

But those questions were minor. Would she feed from him every time they were together? What if she got carried away with sucking his blood? Would he be able to stop her before she drank him dry? He didn't think so. He could end up dead...or a vampire himself, right? How did a person become a vampire anyway?

Whew! Heavy stuff, and now he was getting sleepy. After just one night with her, he was already on her schedule. Up all night, asleep at dawn. But he felt far too sleepy to think seriously about what he should do. See her tomorrow — or run like hell?

* * * * *

Jon watched in amazement, not that he'd ever admit to such a feeling, as Darlene DeMars, his latest submissive, became a swirling mist and left his condo. Then he got into the bed where he'd had her — a vampire! — chained and cuffed just a short time before. The wheels of his mind began to spin as he tried to figure out what the hell just happened to him.

Actually, he'd had to keep his mouth from gaping open in amazement ever since Darlene went into action with those fangs. This was completely abnormal and unacceptable. He'd considered himself beyond any surprises. But a friggin', real live vampire as a sub! Who'd ever believe it? Before tonight, he certainly would have regarded anyone with a story like that as a liar or a total whacko.

But she'd been here, going along with him so easily that he thought he was breaking her in just right.

Hah! Now that he knew the truth, he felt like a blind asshole to have missed all the obvious clues. Like how pale she was—chalking that up to an allergy. She must have been laughing at him inside, thinking he was making a fool of himself.

But then, even after she'd freakin' fed on him, after she told him who she really was, she let him cuff and blindfold her before he fucked her. And she wanted it just the way he was giving it to her. His cock rose in tribute, and Jon reached over to his night table for his special cream, which made a hand job seem like firecrackers going off.

He stroked himself, wishing she were back here. But you go out with vampires, you have to respect the hours they keep. Thoughts of her got his cock harder, and he began to rub stronger, faster.

He'd given her his number. She hadn't committed to seeing him again, but he was sure she would. She really dug the scene, he could tell. And she dug him.

As for him, he wanted to be with her again. Plain and simple. She got to him even before he knew she was a vampire. And once he knew... He closed his fingers tight around his cock, nearly gasping from the pleasure of his hand with the effects of the cream. He rimmed the head with his fingers, imagining Darlene's mouth there.

And her fangs. Did vampires give head? Gave a whole new dimension to "sucking".

Jon's balls tightened, and he felt himself begin to come. He'd come practically a gallon in Darlene. Liked not having to use a condom. Hell, he loved it. Darlene's cunt was so tight and wet around his shaft, he had to really focus to keep from coming in about three seconds. Like he was coming now.

Jon's mind turned off for a few moments as he spurted his cum all over his fingers, onto his belly. He had to see Darlene again. She'd call—she'd had a good time tonight, right? She'd call. But—what if she didn't?

* * * * *

Lynette arrived home all excited to tell Darlene about her night with Nick—okay, all set to brag. Not only did she have the most amazing sex of her life, but Nick was special... And he seemed really to care about her. Heck, Lynette might even admit to Darlene about how she and Nick connected over his volume of *Romeo and Juliet*. Previously, she always pretended to regard Shakespeare's play as sentimental fluff. Now maybe Lynette would confess to Darlene that she wept whenever she saw the play or reread the story.

Speaking of literature, Lynette felt and experienced more than enough tonight to get Veronica on track. And when she told the Comte about her new adventures with Nick, he'd have to tell the Committee to back off. After all, dull and boring people did not fuck gorgeous men they'd just met up their butts.

But where was Darlene? When Lynette first came home, she suspected that her friend might have just turned in early. But after looking all over the house, Lynette realized Darlene wasn't home yet. Her friend had stayed out even later than she had with a guy she'd just met! Lynette gritted her teeth.

Fifteen minutes passed. Dawn was growing uncomfortably close. Lynette paced the floor, worrying about what could have happened to her friend when she went off with that man... Lynette hadn't liked his looks or completely trusted him. What if he...? And then Lynette relaxed. Cripes, Darlene was a *vampire*. There was little that could hurt her. Though getting caught in the sunshine would do some serious damage.

The fact that Darlene was feeling no pain and had experienced no damage became quickly apparent the moment she materialized in the living room, a big fat grin on her face. Darlene looked positively smug. Lynette wondered what the hell she'd been up to.

"I had the most amazing time," Darlene sang, boogying around the room. She paused for a moment. "This place really is a dump, isn't it?"

As Lynette was the one in charge of house maintenance this year — Darlene covered food and bill paying — she slightly resented that remark. Even though she agreed. "Remember? We agreed to keep this place looking shabby — bordering on scary — to keep my relatives from trying to claim the mansion?"

Darlene waved her hands. "No one's bothered us in fifteen years. I think we scared them off permanently. Besides, if anyone comes nosing around, we could always rattle a few chains or something."

Lynette scowled. "Yeah, okay. But I've got more important things to talk about, like having the most phenomenal night..."

Darlene held her hands up to her heart and looked goofy. "Oh, Lynette, mine was fabulous... Things I've been dreaming of for years, but never knew exactly how..."

Oh, no. Darlene was *not* going to top her in this. "I want to tell you about what I did. About Nick LaStrada," she said, not pleased that her voice went soft and mushy at the sound of his name. Darlene would pick up on that.

"Who?" Darlene asked distractedly. Evidently Darlene wasn't picking up on much.

"Nick LaStrada," Lynette growled from between clenched teeth. "My *lover*."

"Right," Darlene sighed. "Mine's named Jon Torrance." She looked around. "I'd love to hear what you have to say, but it really is close to dawn. Time for us to go to bed."

"So it is. But as soon as we wake up, I want to tell you all about what I did. If we can write it up for Veronica—and tell the Comte—all our problems will be solved. Good morning." Lynette started walking up the stairs.

"Wait 'til you hear mine," Darlene said, causing Lynette to turn around and stare at her besotted friend. Darlene waltzed her way to the stairs. "I feel just like Eliza Doolittle in *My Fair Lady*. You know, when she could have danced all night."

"Oh, go to bed," Lynette grumped. Talk about a mood staker.

"I am." Darlene followed her to her bedroom. Lynette swore Darlene was floating so high, she'd have trouble getting her coffin shut.

"Well, I have a date tomorrow night," Lynette said just before she opened her door.

Darlene opened her door and looked smugly at Lynette. "Jon wants a date with me. I took his number. Maybe I'll call him, maybe I'll keep him waiting." She closed her door before Lynette could get the last word. Lynette spent the whole day fuming in her sleep.

* * * * *

Darlene closed her bedroom door before Lynette threw something at it. She didn't usually go in for teasing her friend, but tonight she couldn't resist. Lynette would feel much better when Darlene confessed all the ways tonight had changed her mind and made her see that her friend was sometimes right. Maybe even, in this situation, about the direction they needed to take to revive their Veronica stories. She loved the old Veronica stories. But maybe now it was time for Veronica, like all the rest of them, to change. To get "with it".

As she undressed for her day's sleep, Darlene ran her hands up and down her body. The places Jon touched. She still tingled everywhere. She felt like she'd been asleep for the whole of her existence. Only with Jon had her eyes truly opened.

Now she knew she needed to rest, because tomorrow would bring another important night. Maybe she'd be able to resist calling Jon for a while, but not long. And next time they came together, she'd no longer be the naïve novice he'd consented to take in. Finally, she was one of the adults. She practiced smiling mysteriously.

Funny, before she'd always thought that love looked like lace and roses and sounded like sweet violin music. Tonight, she realized love might carry cuffs and a whip and sound like a subway rattling on its rails.

Love looked like Jon.

Not sure that she'd ever get any sleep, Darlene curled up in her coffin and promptly went under.

* * * * *

Darlene awoke first and was hard at work revising their manuscript before Lynette stumbled downstairs the next night.

"Ready to talk and work?" she asked when Lynette, looking grumpy and rumpled, peered over her shoulder.

"I'm hungry," Lynette croaked.

"Fridge is full," Darlene said, pointing in that general direction.

"More O positive," Lynette muttered, nonetheless heading to the kitchen. Darlene heard the fridge open, and Lynette, despite the complaints, loudly guzzled down a whole pint.

Darlene got up and followed her friend to the kitchen in time to see her wipe her mouth with the back of her hand and burp.

"Last night, I feasted on some AB negative." Her fangs gleamed in the kitchen light. "Made me realize even more dramatically what a rut we've been in. That life is a banquet…"

Darlene held her hand up. "Before you go on, Lynette, I agree."

"You do?" Lynette looked like she'd just had the wind knocked out of her. Probably gathering up steam for a major tirade. Darlene wasn't in the mood.

"Yes." She nodded solemnly. "I have to tell you. Last night I had some prime B negative, and, what with the B positive I had the other night at Club Decadent…well, I've come to the same conclusion. That I've limited us too much, just buying the same old, same old all the time. Pinching those pennies."

Lynette almost smiled.

"I've dropped the ball on the food," Darlene continued.

"I'll say. No wonder we were nominated for that stupid award. You are what you eat..."

Darlene cut her off mid-rant. "I said I've dropped the ball on the *food*." She paused a moment and glared Lynette down when she opened her mouth to speak. With Lynette's full attention on her, Darlene added, "Just like you have on keeping this place in reasonable shape."

Silence. Darlene knew that Lynette did not take criticism well, and might explode in a temperamental hissy fit.

"I hate to admit you're right, but you are," Lynette, her face screwed up like she'd just drunk tainted blood, said at last. Darlene knew what it cost her friend to ever admit she was wrong about anything, and she restrained herself from gloating. Mostly. Though a smug little smile hovered on her lips.

"Go on," Darlene said, her smooth voice belying her inner excitement. She couldn't remember the last time — if ever — that she'd come out on top in an argument with Lynette. To give herself something to occupy her hands — though she'd slaked her hunger earlier — Darlene took a pint of blood from the fridge. Though both she and Lynette had long fallen into the habit of drinking from the plastic beakers they stored blood in, she got one of their crystal goblets from a cabinet, wiped the heavy layer of dust from it, and poured in the O positive. She sat down at the kitchen table and took a sip as she waited for Lynette to continue her tale.

Lynette sat down opposite her friend and shook her head. "It's all about last night." She looked like a teenager who'd just been on her dream date.

"What did you say his name is?"

"Nick," Lynette breathed out. "Nick LaStrada. Would you believe, AB negative?"

"Oh, so you sampled the goodies?"

"Yeah, and he didn't freak out."

"Obviously," Darlene said, amused to see this side of her friend.

"He's coming tonight. Here." Lynette waved her hands in emphasis.

Darlene's eyes widened with surprise. "Here?" She looked around. "Why?" She narrowed her eyes. "Is his place a bigger dump than ours?"

Now Lynette looked rueful, like maybe she regretted her impulse. "Hell, no. The reverse. Neat. It looks like someone who knew what he was doing decorated."

"And you invited him *here*?" Darlene shook her head. She couldn't remember the last time either of them invited anyone to the house. Even well-paid delivery men tended to drop their packages and hightail it off the property.

Lynette shrugged. "I figured if he didn't go shrieking into the night when he found out I was a vampire, this place wouldn't weird him out too much."

Darlene snorted uncharacteristically. "This place weirded out your entire family, three inspectors from the health department, and half the local fire department. Not to mention several police lieutenants. You really think Nick is going to hold up better?"

Now Lynette bit her lip, looking miserable. "I wanted him to really get to know me. You know, lie down in my coffin with me and all."

A tiny niggle of a thought started to rise to Darlene's consciousness. If she didn't know better, she'd suspect her friend, the self-proclaimed queen of the cynical bitches — both before their transformation and since — of being *in love*. Or at least well on her way down that slippery slope. "You want him to share your coffin with you?" she repeated, awe creeping into her voice.

As far as Darlene knew, and she knew pretty much everything there was to be known about her friend, Lynette had never shared her coffin with anyone else before. Lynette was far too private and secretive. Not to mention that sharing a coffin — with a human or another vampire — was considered pretty much the height of intimacy. In some circles, it was regarded as practically tantamount to becoming formally engaged. And Lynette felt she wanted to do this after spending just *one* night with Nick LaStrada?

It must have been one hell of a night! Nick LaStrada must be one hell of a guy. And Lynette looked like Cupid's arrow just found a new target.

Even after all she experienced the night before with Jon Torrance and the tender feelings he evoked in her heart, Darlene hadn't thought about inviting him to their house — let alone, to her coffin. She'd left things pretty open, not even committing for sure to call him. Well, of course she'd call him. But she still wanted to play things cool, so she'd wait 'til midnight. Okay, so her heart started beating faster when she planned out the phone call. Still, it was obvious that she didn't have it anywhere near as bad as Lynette. Thank the universe. One of them had to be clear-eyed enough to keep their goals in view. Like selling Veronica's story again. And, equally important, getting their names disqualified for the contest.

"When did you say Nick was going to come here?" Darlene asked.

"I didn't. But he'll be here at eleven."

Darlene looked over at the clock, which, by some miracle of long-lasting batteries, still functioned. Just past nine. "Hey, that gives us two hours to give the place a quick cleaning."

Lynette looked around her, as if for the first time registering what a pigsty they lived in. "Maybe I should tell him not to come. Two hours isn't nearly enough. Not even with our powers."

"True," Darlene said. "But we don't have to do the whole house. I mean, you're not going to take him into every room, right? Let's see," she began to enumerate on her fingers. "The kitchen, the living room. Those are essential. Being human, he might need to use a bathroom. And, of course, your room. Means each of us takes two rooms, and we have almost an hour to fix each one up."

"You'd do that for me?" Lynette gazed meltingly at Darlene.

Cripes, she did have it bad. "Of course. What are friends for?"

"But I thought you were hot to work on our manuscript."

"Hey, this is an emergency." It was on the tip of her tongue to say something about how far gone Lynette seemed to be, but she decided discretion was the better part of valor here. "Veronica's been waiting this long to get a life. She'll wait a little longer. How about you take your room and the bathroom up there? I'll do the kitchen and the living room."

"I owe you," Lynette said, running off to the ruin of her bedroom.

* * * * *

Two hours later they'd managed to clear away most of the spider webs and mouse pellets, the dust bunnies and the most obvious mold and mildew from the rooms Lynette would let Nick see. She'd also taken a quick bath, sprayed rose scent all over, and dressed in her best underwear and a black silk caftan. She really needed to get some decent clothes, under and outer, she thought as she came downstairs to wait for Nick. Darlene was finishing up a phone conversation.

"Who was that?" Lynette asked. Darlene, looking like she'd just won a supermarket sweep at the blood bank, hung up the receiver.

"Jon." She licked her lips.

"I thought you weren't going to call him 'til midnight."

"So I called him early."

"You're going to leave Nick and me here alone, aren't you?" Lynette asked, almost getting choked up over her friend's thoughtfulness. "You don't have to. This is your house, too."

Darlene shrugged. "Hey, it's not like I don't want to see Jon tonight. Just that I'm going to see him sooner than I planned. He sure sounded glad to hear my voice."

"You won't go 'til Nick arrives, right?"

"You want me to meet him again?"

"Yeah," Lynette said. "Last night at Happy Humping was too fast for either of you to get more than a fleeting glance." She hoped that the two people who mattered most in the world to her would hit it off. The alternative would be too miserable to consider.

Just then the front doorbell, sounding extremely loud and rusty, chimed.

"That must be Nick," Darlene said. "Do you want me to get the door?"

Lynette shook her head. Taking a deep breath, she went to the door and opened it. Nick, looking even more impossibly handsome than she remembered, was standing on the front porch in the total darkness of the night. Damn, they'd forgotten to replace the burned out light bulb. Of course, with her super vision, she could see every detail of how he'd dressed, the small leather tote he carried, and especially the full bouquet of blood-red roses.

Her favorite, she thought, as her heart turned to mush.

"May I come in?" he asked, as Lynette stood blocking the doorway, staring at him.

Had she turned into an idiot or what? "Of course." She stood aside so he could enter. Nick kissed her, a quick sweet greeting, put his tote down on a table, and handed her the roses.

"These are beautiful," she said sniffing the roses, wondering where they'd unearth a suitable vase.

She shouldn't have worried. Darlene, wonderful, brilliant Darlene, was standing in the living room holding a tall blue crystal vase that Lynette didn't even remember having. "I've got some water in here already," were her first words. "What gorgeous flowers!"

"That's Darlene. I know you met her last night, but now you're really meeting her," Lynette said to Nick by way of introduction. "My best friend forever. Darlene DeMars." She turned to Darlene and said, "This is Nick LaStrada. I've told you a little about him."

Darlene held out her hand. "Not nearly enough. Pleased to see you again, Nick."

"I'm honored," Nick said. He was looking around the living room, taking it all in.

"Now I have to run," Darlene said.

"I hope you're not racing off on my account," Nick said.

Darlene shook her head. "Not at all. I've got a date."

"A very lucky guy. Well, I hope to see you again soon," Nick said.

"Me, too."

Darlene hugged Lynette, waved to Nick, and headed off for her second date with Jon.

* * * * *

Darlene's heart hammered with excitement as she raced to grab a cab to take her to Jon's. Though she could have flown, and would have preferred to, it was still fairly early that night, and she was afraid to risk anyone seeing her come down to earth at Jon's building.

She could have taken her time going to Jon's, stringing out his and her anticipation. But now that she was on her way, she couldn't wait to be with him. Fortunately, she caught a cab fairly quickly. And her cabbie seemed preoccupied with his own music, so he didn't try to engage her in conversation. She didn't want any interruptions of her reveries.

Darlene liked Nick. He seemed like he'd be good for Lynette, a real "nice guy". Ironic that Lynette would hook up with Nick while Darlene found herself with a leather-wearing, chain-rattling bad boy. A delicious bad boy in every sense of the words.

Darlene licked her lips. What did Jon have planned for tonight? Her pussy got moist. She wished the cabbie would drive faster.

* * * * *

What was she supposed to do next? Lynette realized that, as hostess, she should offer Nick something to eat or drink. But all they had in the house was O positive. Shit! She hadn't thought this through. She should have gotten some wine and pretzels or something humans liked to snack on. She would next time, if there was going to be a next time. Nick seemed surprised as he surveyed the living room.

"Sorry, I don't have any wine or goodies to offer you." Lynette mentally kicked herself for starting off the evening with a fucking apology.

"I don't need any refreshments," Nick said, his voice deep and throaty. He looked like he'd gotten a haircut today and smelled like fresh woodsy aftershave — and hot AB negative.

"This is quite a place you have here," he said as she led him over to the loveseat, the same one the Comte dusted off before sitting on. No clouds of dust rose when Nick sat, and Lynette thanked her stars. Darlene must have vacuumed or something.

Lynette sat close to Nick, savoring his warmth. "Not decorated nearly as nicely as yours."

"I'm not into making comparisons." He put his arm around her shoulders and pulled her closer. "Lots of antiques here. I like that, though maybe the place is a little on the dark side."

The dark side? It was like a morgue after a major power failure, but Lynette didn't want to break the growing mood with one of her sarcastic remarks. "Those aren't antiques. Just old furniture. Darlene and I haven't done much here in ages... Long story."

"And I'd love to hear it, but I've been dying all day to be with you."

"Not literally?" Lynette wondered if maybe she had drunk too much of his good, rich blood the night before.

He put his head back and laughed loud and deep, with Lynette joining him. "No, definitely not. I've never before felt as alive as I have all day today." And then he cupped her chin in his hand and looked deep in her eyes. Lynette felt like he could read everything about her on her face, like he knew all her secrets and every step of her voyage from where she'd been to where she was now.

Chapter Seven

From Veronica Vampira's Secret Diaries:
My love will bring to me his trusty tools of the lover's trade.
First will be a bountiful bouquet of brightly blooming blossoms,
releasing their aromatic fragrance to fill the air with romance.
Second will be a well-worn volume of love poems, a book he
searched painstakingly for in the ancient bowels of used book
stores. Last, but never least, will be his powerful, strong, well-
muscled arms, to hold me near his rapidly beating-for-me heart.

Nick brought her to him, and his lips began a gentle exploration of hers that rapidly deepened in intensity. Lynette melted into Nick's arms at the same time that every sense and nerve sprang to full attention. She felt her fangs descend into position as all of her hungers pushed to the forefront. She quickly realized that no matter how much she fed before she was with Nick, being in his arms would cause her body to react like she was coming off a three-day fast.

Fearing that he'd hurt himself on her fangs, Lynette backed off for a moment. Nick, his brow furrowed, asked what was wrong. In reply, she smiled sheepishly, her mouth open enough for him to glimpse the fangs. "I don't want you to get hurt," she said hoarsely.

"If I do, you'll kiss it and make it better, right?" Nick asked, his eyes now hooded with his own desires. "Like you did last night after you fed off me." His voice sounded slightly quavery. "When you licked my punctures with your tongue."

"Yes, I guess I can."

"No need to worry. Is it your tongue or your saliva that heals?" Nick stroked her face with his fingers, his lips close to hers.

"The saliva."

"Good for whatever ails you." Nick boldly plunged his tongue back into her mouth.

Now that she knew he wasn't worried, Lynette relaxed into the kiss. Nick, never breaking the kiss, arranged her legs over his lap—into full contact with his raging erection. By now Lynette's nipples were two hard pebbles jutting up against her bra. Her pussy, vibrating with desire, grew moist and soft.

"I need more of you," Nick moaned. In moments they were both stretched out face to face on the narrow couch. He pulled her to him, smothering her lips with his probing kiss, and her breasts flattened against his hard chest. Lynette could see his little brown nipples, now budded tightly as hers. She longed to taste him there, and she wanted him to suck her breasts. But stronger urges beckoned.

Lynette slipped up her caftan and opened her powerful legs around his, closing the distance between them, so she could jam her pussy up against the hard ridge of his penis. Between his huge cock and the teeth of the zipper stroking her clit and her wet, wet folds through the silk of the only good panties she owned, Lynette thought she was about to die again from sheer ecstasy.

Her rational self said they should get naked, that she hadn't yet had the chance to take him up to her coffin.

With little effort, she shut that rational self up and angled herself even tighter against Nick.

He clutched her ass and howled out his desire for her, matching her stroke for stroke as the two of them humped madly on the couch. Lynette was pistoning her hips, arching, thrusting, thrashing to feel him everywhere. She burned and ached for his divine friction, touching her clit and every place she needed him as his big hands stroked her ass.

And then, their arms and legs still entangled, they both flew off the couch, stopping their frenetic humping for just a moment as the surprise of landing on the floor registered. And then they resumed, rolling across the living room floor in their frantic need for contact.

"Nick, oh Nick," Lynette cried out as she began to come. She felt like she was trembling all over, totally out of control, totally out of the universe with the sheer amazing pleasure of the release that was shaking her.

"Lynette, good Christ," Nick called out, holding her ever tighter. He was moments behind her in his own orgasm, his still zippered cock throbbing and bursting against her wide-open pussy.

She couldn't help it. She had to feed from him now, or she'd expire into a lump of quivering ash right here at his feet. With a gasp and a sob, Lynette sank her fangs into Nick's amazing neck. It was hard to know whose heart was hammering harder as she slaked her monumental thirst with his precious blood. More delicious than she'd remembered.

With great effort, Lynette drew back from Nick, who looked almost as dazed as he had the night before, though now he knew what was going on. Lynette had hypnotized him enough so that the feeding pleasured him. But now, before she tongued him to seal up the wound, she wanted him to feel those punctures, to fully know what was really going on between them.

Gazing into his eyes, wanting to know everything going on in his heart and soul at this very moment, Lynette reached for Nick's hand and raised his fingers to his neck. With great deliberation, she positioned his fingers so he could touch the holes she'd just made.

A flicker of pain flashed in Nick's eyes before his eyelids lowered. "Please heal me now." His voice sounded faint and far away.

Lynette wordlessly ran her tongue over the punctures. Nick healed exceptionally quickly. In less than a minute, his bite marks had disappeared so completely that she could scarcely see the faint outline that remained.

They lay together wordlessly on the floor for the longest while. Lynette suspected that Nick had fallen asleep, which wasn't a surprising reaction to being fed on. She was growing cold and a bit stiff. The moment she began to stir, Nick fuzzily asked, "Where are you going?"

"I don't know about you, but pleasant as this is, I don't intend to lie on the floor all night." She stood up and pulled the now very wrinkled caftan down over her legs.

Looking like a boy who'd just been caught with the whole cookie jar behind his back, Nick smiled and sat up. He seemed as though he was trying to get his bearings before he got completely vertical. "Good God, Lynette. That was so amazing. I haven't dry-humped since high school. I forgot how delicious it can be."

"Is that what we were doing?"

"Yeah."

"Now I understand why that place is called Happy Humping," Lynette said. Then, turning serious, she asked, "Are you okay, Nick?"

He frowned. "What do you mean?"

She pursed her lips. "I did feed pretty passionately from you."

A flicker of discomfort passed over his face, and Lynette wondered if he wasn't a lot less comfortable with her being a vampire than he said. But he smiled and answered, "Oh, I'm more than fine. Finer than I've ever been before."

"Great. Because I need to know that you'd tell me if that's not the case, if something was really wrong..."

He grinned. "I expect you'd know if something was wrong. And you told me yesterday that nothing would go wrong."

"Yeah," she said, "but you get me so hot, I forget. And I am only human..." She slapped herself upside the head as she said the last words. An illustration of exactly how much she sometimes forgot herself, especially in the throes of the passion Nick inspired.

The both laughed, defusing some of the tension Lynette felt had begun to seep into the room.

"I never did get to show you some of the rest of the house." Lynette pulled Nick to his feet.

"How big is this place?"

Lynette chuckled. The house was so large, neither she nor Darlene ever thought about many of the rooms and kept the doors to them shut. "Very. We have seven bedrooms upstairs, each with its own bath, plus an office. Down here, there's the kitchen, breakfast room, formal dining room, living room, den, playroom, and three offices."

"Three offices downstairs?"

"Yeah. Maybe a little indulgent. Darlene and I each have our own, then we have one where we work together on our Veronica stories. Come, I want to take you upstairs." She took his hand and began leading him.

"You gonna show me the whole house?"

Talk about scaring him. "Maybe some other time. Right now, I want to show you my bedroom."

"As in a real bedroom with a bed and all?" Nick asked as he followed her.

Lynette laughed. "Yes, there is a real bed."

"Is that where you sleep—or whatever you call it—during the day?"

"We call it sleep," Lynette said. "Or rest. We still keep using the same language we did before…" They'd reached the top of the steps and were in the middle of the long hallway that extended from the staircase. Lynette had the room immediately to the right of the stairs, Darlene the room on the left.

Lynette had left the door to her room closed. Now as she stood poised to open it to Nick, she felt her first attack of nerves. How was he going to react to seeing her inner sanctum, the place where she spent so much of her existence?

"So you sleep in a bed?" Nick looked curious and just a bit wary.

"Not exactly. More like *on* the bed." She opened the door with a flourish.

Lynette's room was large. She'd hung a painting of a lighthouse at Point Reyes on one of the teal blue walls, along with white lace curtains—now dusty and stiff with age—at the large windows. And, of course, total blackout shades. Lynette crossed the room and closed the black velvet drapes over the windows. Several rag rugs scattered across the polished wooden floor added the only other color immediately apparent.

Lynette had a king-size bed—no headboard or footboard—centered on the wall between the two large windows. And diagonally across the bed—a huge polished mahogany coffin, now closed.

Nick gulped hard, and Lynette could sense his nervousness. She tried to remember how the sight of a coffin affected her when she was human, but couldn't bring back any recollections of anxiety. Still, she must have had them. Looking at him, she wanted to rush over and assure him that a coffin was just another kind of space. Nothing inherently scary about it. But first she wanted Nick to get his bearings so he could feel receptive to what she was going to say.

"Do you want to touch it?" she asked.

* * * * *

A mix of emotions he couldn't begin to separate crashed and exploded in Nick's head. Fear, lust, revulsion, love, confusion, and did he mention fear? Everything about being with Lynette was totally weird. And wonderful. Hell, maybe a coffin was one of the saner parts. At least it was real, not a hallucination.

'Til the coffin part, he could tell himself he was imagining the vampire shtick—a fantasy induced by great sex and a fabulous actress. But this coffin wouldn't disappear when he touched it. This was the reality of being involved with Lynette, a woman he was starting to have some intense feelings for.

He hesitated for another moment, and then nodded. Nick reached out and slowly stroked the glossy polished finish of the coffin. "This is really beautifully made," he said, a hint of longing in his voice.

"Much nicer than the one I had when I first became a vampire."

"Oh, really?" He looked up at Lynette, who was standing on the other side of the coffin across from him. "What kind did you have then?"

"Plain, unvarnished pine," she said ruefully. "The cheapest kind. No lining inside, nothing."

He looked into the coffin, which was lined in deep purple silk. One of the most expensive and luxurious kinds made she told him.

"You know, I treated myself using the royalties Darlene and I made from the Veronica Vampira stories during their heyday."

"This must have cost a fortune." He touched the wood again.

"It did. Worth every penny." From the moment each dawn when she stretched out in the coffin, to the moment when she arose each night, Lynette told him she savored the soft whispery feel of the fine silk against her skin.

"It looks quite...sumptuous," Nick said. He shook his head. "I have to tell you, Lynette. I'm experiencing some major cognitive dissonance here—or something. I mean I'm in a beautiful woman's bedroom, standing across from her, and we're talking about a *coffin*, for Christ's sake. A fucking *coffin*."

"Yes, we are."

He snorted, raising his hands up and waving them dismissively in the air. "You don't even want to know how far out of my depth I feel right now. Like I've landed on a frigging alien planet in some other dimension with the most amazing woman I've ever met in my life."

"If you landed on the planet, you'd be the alien," Lynette pointed out gently.

"Don't confuse me with logic," Nick snorted.

"The coffin freaks you out," Lynette said sadly.

He nodded. "It does. Oh, yeah, big time. It does. Lynette I'm sorry, but it does." He looked down then looked over at her. "Why did you bring me up here?"

"I wanted you to try out the coffin, to lie in there with me."

He recoiled. "But it's so *narrow*. And I'd be afraid of suffocating." Maybe this was the time to call a halt to what was coming at him too fast, too hard.

But leaving her was even harder than staying. She looked like she was about to beg. How could he resist?

* * * * *

She sensed that she was turning him off big time. "I don't mean we should close the top the way I do during the day." She was afraid that maybe she'd lose Nick over the reality of what the coffin was in her life. But she wasn't going to give up that easily. After all, if her feeding off him didn't freak him out, why should a mere coffin do so? "And Nick, it's not as narrow as you might think. Look. It's deeper and wider than standard—one of the deluxe features of this model."

"Do you really expect me to try it out?" He reached out and touched the coffin.

"Do you want to open it and feel the lining?"

Nick pulled his hand back. Lynette rolled her eyes. "For Pete's sake. It's just like trying out a mattress in a store. No big deal. But if you don't want to experience it, we can go back downstairs."

Nick seemed to give himself up to some internal debate. Lynette waited patiently, hoping he would say yes. Because she knew if he refused to at least try lying in the coffin, it was all over between them. The coffin was too important a part of who she was for her to try to be in a relationship with a man who totally refused any contact with it. She wasn't even going to mention now her fantasy of the two of them making love in the coffin, or remind him that he'd asked what her fantasy was the other night. She hadn't been able to come up with an answer then. But since she got up that night, she'd been thinking about what it would be like to have her lair filled with the scent of their sex together, and her pussy creamed at the thought. However, if he was being so edgy about even stretching out inside...

Nick appeared lost in thought, and Lynette tried not to hover. "Okay," Nick said at last. "I'll try it. But just for five seconds. Then I'm out of there."

Lynette practically sagged to her knees in relief. He would try. That meant she could continue being with him. Maybe she didn't even have to abandon her fantasy of having sex in the coffin with him tonight. But one thing at a time.

Nick got up on the bed and knelt next to the coffin. "I never thought I'd climb into one of these under my own power," he said. Lynette was relieved that his sense of humor—or of adventure—seemed to be returning.

"How do you get into this?" He laughed nervously.

"When it's on the bed like that, knees first works well for me," Lynette said, pulling closer to Nick.

With a brief shudder, Nick climbed into the coffin. After a minimum of fuss and fidgeting, he was able to stretch out. After a moment or two, he even appeared to relax.

"How are you doing in there?" Lynette asked when five seconds had elapsed.

"You were right. It's deeper and wider than I thought it would be. More peaceful, somehow. And the silk lining is great, very luxurious."

Now Lynette let go of some of the tension she'd begun to feel. Nick seemed to accept the coffin after all. "See? I told you."

"But there is one problem," Nick said.

"What's that?" Lynette wondered what he'd come up with.

"It's awfully lonely in here. Why don't you squeeze in here with me?"

Better than what she was expecting him to say after the rocky start. Suppressing her whoop of joy, Lynette climbed in on top of Nick, who had more than ample room to lift his arms and put them around her. "Thank you," she said.

"I'm the one who should thank you," Nick whispered back. "For being so patient with me when I start getting all neurotic."

"You're doing fine. Just fine." As Nick's erection pushed up against her belly, Lynette realized just how well he was doing.

"Let's make love," he whispered, thrusting up to her.

Wow! It was like he'd read her mind about wanting to make love in her coffin. Or maybe it was his life force asserting itself in the face of death and all. Whatever, she was never one to look a gift horse in the mouth, so to speak.

"Yes, but this time, let's get naked first," she said. Delicious as the humping had been, she wanted skin to skin this time.

"I guess we'll have to climb back out to do that," he said. "Unless you know some magic or something."

"You overestimate me."

"No, I certainly do not."

She got out of the coffin first, and he quickly followed. Like he'd been climbing out of coffins forever.

"I have one more request," Lynette said.

"Your wish is my command." He bowed down to her.

"I like that. Could you do that bow again?"

He complied, going even deeper. "So what is it you want?"

"Seeing as how we landed on the floor before, maybe we'd be better off getting the coffin off the bed and on the floor to start with."

His eyes lit up. "I'm impressed. Not only gorgeous, but brilliant. I'd hate to think what would happen to your coffin if we crashed it to the floor *in flagrante...*"

"It would mess up the finish."

He got serious for a moment. "Uh, Lynette, seriously. What would happen if your coffin were damaged?"

She smiled. This guy really was a worrier. Like Darlene. What was it about her that attracted worriers? "You remember that pine box I told you about?"

He nodded.

"Well, I still have that and two or three other backups." She put her hand on the coffin. "This one's my favorite, but it's not my only. But you're right. I still wouldn't want it to get messed up."

The two of them lifted the coffin and set it flat on the floor, away from any of the other furniture and rag rugs. Then Nick remembered something. "I got you a gift," he said. "But I left it downstairs in my tote bag."

"A gift? In addition to the roses?" Lynette asked. She loved gifts, and she really wanted to see what Nick had come up with. "Is it something you want me to have before we make love?"

Nick grinned, evidently pleased with himself when he saw her delight. "Definitely. I'll run downstairs and get it."

Within moments, he was back carrying the tote bag. "I didn't get it wrapped or anything." He extracted a double-headed dildo.

"Oh, God, thank you. No wrapping necessary." Lynette couldn't imagine any other gift he might have gotten her that would have made her feel happier—or more excited. As she looked at it and ran her fingers over all the contours, her pussy contracted in a spasm of pure delight. "Thank you, thank you," she said. "Do I need a harness with this one?"

"Not sure, but I got one," he said. "I think using the harness will make it easier to get the dildo into your pussy and then position it in my ass—and let the fun and games begin. Of course, doing this in the coffin is going to add...another dimension."

As he said these last words with an edge in his voice, Lynette couldn't help wondering if he'd changed his mind.

"No, I want very much to love you in your coffin," he said, as he began taking off her clothes.

Though Lynette had had sex in coffins in the early days, it had been ages since the last time. And never in her own. More importantly, Lynette realized what a milestone tonight was. This would be the first time she ever shared this—her favorite coffin—with a lover.

As she watched Jon strip down to glorious nakedness, Lynette felt shaken by the momentousness of what she was about to do. If she still drank champagne, now would be the time to break out the vintage stuff.

Champagne? Hell, next she'd be drawing little hearts with her and Nick's initials in them. If she didn't know better, she'd swear she was turning into Darlene—a quivering, sentimental blob who actually wanted Veronica to make her own Valentine's cards and hang red paper hearts in her window panes.

Nick stood in front of her, his cock jutting out powerfully, his eyes gleaming and his arms open to her. Nick was doing this to her—turning her soft and gooey. Like a woman in love.

Lynette shoved that thought away as fast as she could. It bounced back. Wouldn't Darlene laugh her head off if she ever found out? How could she hide her feelings from Darlene, who knew her far too well?

Well, Lynette wasn't going to let worry over this rob her or detract from her time with Nick. Just the sight and feel of the double-headed dildo set her pussy to twitching. Nick held the detailed rubber dildo out to her.

"We'll need lubrication and condoms," he said. "I guess we should put them on the dildo before we climb in."

Sounded so prosaic, but the whole operation took on a sensuous thrill, raising Lynette's arousal level. Nick held the dildo while Lynette rolled on the condoms, then spread the cream. He looked down into the coffin at the purple silk lining, then back over at her. "Are you sure we're really going to be able to do this?"

She didn't want to tell him she'd done it before, in narrower coffins. "This one's an extra wide."

He still looked a tad doubtful. "We might have to go into some interesting contortions."

"Worth it." She looked from him to the dildo and back. If her pussy got any wetter, it might dissolve. Nick climbed into the coffin and stretched out flat on his belly. She rubbed some cream into the crack of Nick's ass.

Lynette knew his erection was smooshed into the silk lining at the bottom, and she felt a shiver of delicious arousal knowing his fully engorged cock was imprinting her bed with its feel and scent.

There was just enough room for her to get her knees between Nick's legs and the sides of the coffin. She bent down and licked him, from the nape of his neck to the start of his crack. He shuddered deliciously. With his head turned to the side, his groan was loud and clear.

Lynette had to admit it was going to be tricky to position the dildo exactly right and then get into a satisfying mutual rhythm. Tricky, but worth it. Now she was grateful that her vampire nature gave her extra powers of flexibility. Something she'd have over any of his previous lovers, and probably any future ones, too. The notion brought an edge of sadness, which Lynette promptly banished.

She figured first she'd put the dildo in herself, then into Nick. After four tries, Lynette had to admit that, even for her, the angle of the dangle was just not going to work. Nick, meanwhile, kept moaning out his appreciation for all her efforts.

Careful to keep the condoms on the dildo, Lynette felt them to see if she needed to apply more cream. So far so good. Next she tried inserting the dildo into Nick first, then herself. This time she gave up after three tries.

Then she had a brainstorm. Much as she wanted a great imprint of Nick's cock in the silk, she had to get them both into a more conducive position.

"Nick, get on your knees."

Judging from the small thrusts of his tush while he'd been on his belly, Nick had already been getting a little friction going between his penis and the silk. Lynette smiled, knowing she'd sense his sex energy later, when she slept. Nick grunted, complying a bit awkwardly. He took up lots of the room in the coffin, but Lynette was able to position herself exactly where she wanted to now. Nick bent over the coffin edge so that his ass came right up to her hips. She had her legs spread over his butt, the dildo perfectly in place to please them both.

Holding on tight for their wild ride, Lynette began to buck, moving the dildo in and out of Nick's ass as her pussy muscles played with her part of it. Though the dildo couldn't compete with how great Nick's cock felt in her, for second best it was pretty damned good. If she angled herself just so, the dildo hit all the places she needed, and wanted, for it to touch. Though she wasn't moaning nearly as loudly as Nick, she held up her part of the chorus the two of them made.

Nick was thrusting his butt up, in total sync with Lynette's rhythm. His erect cock now swung with each arc the two of them made. He began to stroke his cock with one hand, which evidently got old fast as he needed both hands to support himself. Lynette, whose hands were free, was more than happy to take over.

She closed the fingers of one hand around his cock, and Nick cried out. With her other hand, she cupped his balls and gave a good squeeze. Cripes, she realized that, between the two of them, they had three cocks. Three cocks in a coffin—a new love song. Nick's cock was so warm and alive. Though the dildo felt amazing, nothing could turn her on like Nick, pulsing with energy in her hand. Every time she stroked him, the touch echoed in her throbbing clit. Nick responded to each caress of her fingers, deepening her pleasure in being together like this. She nibbled on his shoulder, savoring all the ways the two of them were connecting.

"Lynette," he moaned. "Oh, God, I've never felt anything like this before. I love you."

Lynette was so shocked by his pronouncement, she almost stopped what she was doing. Except that it felt too damned good.

He said he loved her. She wasn't dumb enough to think it was real. After all, weren't men in the throes of passion known to say those three words that were making her heart jump up and down—and later declare they didn't mean anything?

She was going to come. Lynette didn't know if this was because of their lovemaking or his words or all of it taking place together—blowing the top off her head.

"Oh, God," he howled as he began to come—his seed spilling onto her hand, splashing him and pouring onto the silk lining. And then she shrieked out her climax. Quivering, she put her arms around him and reclined along his back.

After Nick recovered and realized where his cum went, he apologized. "I'm getting this all over your lining."

Lynette chuckled dryly. She reluctantly moved away from her comforting perch, took her hand, and spread the rest of his cum on the sides and bottom of the coffin. She licked whatever residue was left off her fingers. Nuzzling Nick from behind, she eventually removed the dildo from both of them. Then she climbed out of the coffin, and he joined her. Still half erect despite his massive orgasm, Nick pulled her into his arms.

"Thank you," she said.

He looked at her in surprise. "Thank *you*, Lynette, oh thank *you*." He pulled her head to his chest, where she heard the thundering of his heart.

He dressed quickly, and, though she'd have preferred to stay naked with him, she followed his lead.

Once they were both dressed, he cupped her chin in his hand and turned her head up. "I have another gift for you."

Lynette couldn't believe it. He'd already given her one gift and they'd just made love in her coffin, more than fulfilling her fantasy. "Something else? Oh Nick, I could get used to this."

Except he looked so sad. Why did he look sad? He reached into his tote bag and handed her his copy of *Romeo and Juliet*. The one they'd read together the night before.

Lynette was speechless. He was giving her his special copy of the play they both loved? "Thank you." That was all she could come up with. She'd cherish this book forever.

"I'm so sorry."

"For what?" How could he hand her a gift like this and say he was sorry?

"That was beautiful," he said, "but this has to be the end between us."

Talk about having freezing water flung over her. "I don't understand."

"I really came here tonight intending to give you the gifts and then leave."

Lynette's senses reeled with shock. "You mean you knew you were going to break up with me when you arrived? What changed your mind?"

He looked sheepish. "Look. This is all going too deep and too fast for me. Lynette, I can't go on being with you. You'll ruin me for other women…"

Of course, she thought. She shouldn't have expected a wonderful man like Nick to want to be with her on any kind of long-term basis. He'd want a normal relationship with a normal woman. Freaks like her needn't apply.

Still fresh and hot from sex, Lynette felt at a disadvantage. Of course, Nick was also fresh and hot. But he was the one steering their words. And that didn't seem to give him any discomfort.

"I understand." She willed herself not to get teary and mushy. "What's the saying? It's been real. See you around…"

Nick bit his lip. "I'll never forget you."

"Nor I you," Lynette said. "Much as I'll try." An attempt at a little humor. Very little. Hadn't he just told her he loved her a few short minutes ago? Hah! It was all a crock, just like she'd always told Darlene. Lynette visualized herself strong and invincible, a goddess on a white horse. For pity's sake, horses were scared to death of her. As this man should have had the good sense to be too.

She drew herself up to her full height and began peering at him with her vampire glare. "I guess you'd better go now." She pointed in the general direction of the front door.

"God, Lynette, if only you knew how sorry I am. If only you were…"

"Yeah, and if wishes were horses and all that." Why'd she have horses on the brain? "Just go, Nick. Have a good life."

He was fully dressed by now. He bent to kiss her once more, but she turned her face away.

He shrugged. "I know you're pissed as hell now, but I hope you'll be able to forgive me. And that you'll never forget me."

She watched him leave, and suddenly became aware of how empty and quiet the house was. Darlene would be home soon. They'd talk. In the meantime, Lynette pulled out their rejected Veronica manuscript and began to work.

Then she put the papers aside and gave herself up to her tears.

Chapter Eight

From Veronica Vampira's Secret Diaries:
My one unique true prince is manly and masculine, but has the
refined, sensitive sensibilities of a penniless, poverty-stricken
poet painfully impaled upon the sharpened, pointy teeth of the
eternal dilemma of the ongoing, relentless search for love and
meaning in the harsh, heartless reality of the real world...

When Darlene took off for Jon's condo, she was glad Lynette had Nick there with her. It would have made her sad to leave Lynette alone. The chemistry between her friend and the new man in her life was so strong, Darlene could practically smell it. The two of them would have been polite but extremely frustrated if Darlene had planned to stick around.

Now as she took the private elevator up to Jon's condo, Darlene found her curiosity and her arousal begin to rise. What did Jon have planned for her tonight? He more than hinted that she had lots to learn about the scene. And, of course, about being a submissive. She liked that Jon was so clearly a dominant, and that he'd had so much experience. Quite by accident—or was it?—she'd fallen into the hands of the perfect teacher for her. More than a teacher.

Jon was waiting for Darlene when the elevator arrived at his penthouse. *Not.* She might have wished for that, but Darlene had to admit to herself that waiting at the door for his date was so not Jon's style. And, she also realized, this was part of what appealed to her about Jon.

Instead, the moment she stepped off the elevator, Jon's voice issued forth from some hidden loudspeaker, momentarily startling Darlene. "Now that you're here, proceed to my front door, which is unlocked. Let yourself in. I'm waiting...most impatiently."

Whatever electronic goodies Jon had put in place for this welcome impressed Darlene. She suppressed a brief laugh at the thought of him unlocking the door for her. As if any lock could have kept her out... But this was yet another way for Jon to at least maintain some illusion of mastering her. Darlene liked and respected him for putting so much energy into being in charge. All her nerve endings, especially the ones in her groin, began to tingle in anticipation as she turned the knob of his door.

The entrance, and all Darlene could easily see when she opened the door, was pleasantly dark, lit by the flames of what seemed to be several hundred musk-scented candles. Romantic. Darlene didn't immediately see Jon.

"Come into the living room," he said. "I'm waiting for you."

Oh, and she was waiting for him, too. Darlene slipped off her cloak, hanging it on one of the hooks near the front door. Then, squaring her shoulders, she walked into the living room.

Jon was standing straight and solid, his arms open to pull her into an embrace. "At last," he murmured. "At last."

Darlene thought she detected a note of tenderness in his voice, and she nearly turned to jelly. Thank God he immediately straightened and backed off. "I got a new toy today, and I want to try it out with you."

New toy, Darlene thought. With a man like Jon, those words could encompass a wide gamut. "What new toy?"

He grinned wickedly. "I'll show you in a moment. But first, do you want to pick a new safe word tonight?"

"No," she said. "I think *editor* is still a good choice for stopping anything."

"*Editor* it is." He moved away from her to take a small black leather box off one of the large glass cubes that served as end tables. He extracted what looked like a pair of skimpy thong panties made of thin leather straps. The piece that would go over her pussy lips looked like a butterfly with something attached to it.

"What's that?" Darlene asked. It didn't look like any sort of whip or spanking device.

"Get undressed and put this on, now."

"But what is it?"

Jon's eyebrows drew together in a fierce scowl, and he delivered two stinging smacks on her rear. Darlene's fangs began to descend, but she used all her will to halt the process. It was far too early for her fangs to come into tonight's scene, and she'd vowed to constrain her normal vampiric responses.

"I'll give you the information you need when I'm ready, and not before. Now put this on." The leather dangled from his outstretched hand, swinging slightly.

"I need to get undressed first."

"Yes, of course. I want you to put this on, and then I'm going to cuff you."

Darlene was going to ask if the cuffing would be like yesterday's, then remembered she was not to ask questions. Though she wouldn't have minded feeling his hand on her butt again, she decided to play along with his script right now—and not ask any of the questions she was burning to.

She quickly shrugged off her clothing and stood before him. Jon swept his eyes over her, then handed her the gizmo. Darlene stepped into the thong, which felt like a harness. A piece of hard plastic that fit into her pussy slit and nudged her clit formed part of the butterfly ornament. Darlene gave a little wiggle, savoring a sensation that nearly set her teeth on edge with sheer pleasure.

Jon appeared pleased with how the thong fit Darlene. That made two of them. She wondered if tonight was going to be more pleasure—and less pain—than the previous night, and surprised herself by feeling a jolt of disappointment at the possible absence of pain. She should have known better. She was with Jon, after all.

"I also want you to wear these." He indicated a pair of black open-toed, slingbacks with five-inch heels. She stepped into them, amazed that they were exactly the right size. But then, she shouldn't have expected less than perfection in anything that had to do with Jon.

With the heels on, the top of Darlene's head came to Jon's eye level. Perfect position for nibbling on his neck. Her fangs tingled again. Sometime tonight, she'd be feeding again.

Jon ran his hand over each inch of the leather, making careful note of how the straps hugged her body. He mumbled some words to himself, which Darlene, even with her exquisite hearing, couldn't quite make out. Now he motioned her to walk back and forth, like a runway model at a most exclusive showing. Much as she enjoyed the stroke of the butterfly as she moved, Darlene wanted more.

Jon picked up the box and said, "We need to go to my bedroom for the rest."

The bedroom already? That sounded great. As Darlene walked with Jon, she felt a sizzling tingle zigzag up and down her slit, putting her clit into high vibration mode—and she nearly stumbled. Jon smacked her tush again.

She felt confused. What produced that sharp sensation, that irresistible tingle? Was it from the way her legs nudged the butterfly to rub her pussy as she walked? The sensation felt too intense to result from such a simple movement. And when she continued on into the bedroom, the pleasure was less sharp.

Now Jon looked smug. "On your back," he commanded.

Darlene lay down and looked at Jon, waiting for the next direction. She still had the shoes on. Jon took them off—and Darlene wondered whether she'd be wearing them for more than walking a few steps.

"Spread your arms and legs out wide as you can," Jon barked. She opened her arms and legs into two large vees. With her legs so wide open, the butterfly's stimulation diminished—a disappointment.

Jon took less time cuffing her than he had yesterday. When he had her exactly as he seemed to want her, Jon stepped back like an artist admiring his landscape. Then he picked up what Darlene could now see was a small cylinder from the leather box her thong came from and gave a big squeeze.

A jolt of earthquake proportions slammed through Darlene's pussy, and she came within inches of breaking her bonds and flying to the ceiling. A shred of sanity and the cessation of the jolt brought Darlene back to the bed. "What the hell?" she panted, lapsing into a rare profanity.

Jon smacked the bottom of her feet with the heel of one of her shoes, but his heart mustn't have been fully in it because the blow barely hurt. "When are you going to remember—no questions?"

Darlene expected that she wasn't supposed to answer, so she kept silent. But her fangs throbbed in anticipation.

After several beats of silence, Jon said, "I will give you all the information you need, when I determine you should have it. Not before. And if you ask me, I will postpone telling you. I hope that's clear. You can answer now."

"It is." She figured that was the response he wanted, and also the one that would get her some answers.

He nodded perfunctorily and held up the cylinder. "I want to play some more, and it looks like this new toy has lots of potential. What I'm holding here is a plain old ordinary remote control—the kind men all over the world use for various forms of nightly pleasure."

The only remote controls she'd ever known about were the ones people used for TV and videos. That was not what Jon was talking about here.

"This remote control is attached to the butterfly in your cunt." Jon gave it a slight squeeze which produced a pleasing warmth along her pussy lips. Darlene wiggled her hips slightly to give herself up to the sensation.

Jon then squeezed harder, and Darlene was once again nearly propelled up out of the bed, the jolt producing a more intense focus on her most sensitive parts than she'd ever felt before. She was on the verge of screaming out her confusion at the incredible pleasure when Jon eased up. She seriously doubted that she could handle much more of that focused stimulation without breaking her bonds and causing serious damage to the room — and possibly to Jon. But she couldn't tell him any of this, or she'd impair the progress of the scene and ruin Jon's new toy.

To hell with the butterfly. She was beginning to think *she* was Jon's new toy. And for right this moment, 'til she was ready to spring free and appease her hunger and thirst, that was exactly what she wanted.

If she could live through it. Okay, survive it. It would take all her strength of will and every last drop of determination to keep herself imprisoned here if he was going to subject her to the biggest jolt of stimulation. And Jon probably knew this.

Ridiculous as it was for her to cut herself off from using her powers, Darlene knew it was the only way for her to be with Jon. And that was what she wanted. Along with getting this expert tour of sex toys and how to use them. In this area, she was probably centuries ahead of Lynette already. Once the two of them finally got back to their writing, they would produce manuscripts that knocked their editor's socks off.

Editor. Her safe word. She wasn't going to go there now. She was going to get through whatever Jon had planned for her tonight without breaking out — one way or another.

"You get the drift. With this remote, I can make that butterfly stimulate your cunt from zero to a hundred. And with you cuffed, and with the way you're going to move each time I press a button, well… Darlene, I'm going to record you on video and with a digital camera set to take automatic snaps."

Cameras? Jon was so knowledgeable—surely he had to know she wouldn't register on any film. At most, the cameras would record the rattling of the chains that attached her cuffs to the bed. Not wanting him to be disappointed, Darlene risked telling him. "Jon, those cameras aren't going to be able to record anything."

He narrowed his eyes at her, then pursed his lips in self-disgust. "Shit! I *knew* that."

Darlene braced herself for a blow, which didn't come. For a moment, she feared he'd be turned off enough to just end their evening—and maybe cut off any future relationship between them.

Instead, Jon muttered to himself, "I need to invent a film that *can* record vampires. It must be possible."

Darlene wasn't about to tell him that many had tried, and no one had found it possible yet. Though she was hardly expert on vampire history, even she knew that much. But Jon's eyes began to gleam as the thought came to him, and Darlene now clearly understood why her lover was so successful at his work.

"Did you invent this, uh, apparatus we're using now?" Darlene asked.

Jon arched an eyebrow. "Don't try to distract me." And he gave a huge, vicious jab to the control. Darlene's legs twitched as much as they could as the pleasure shot through her whole body, which now felt centered and concentrated on her pussy. Darlene had a momentary mental image of her clit, which felt like it was swelling and growing and would soon take over the bedroom, then San

Francisco and the world. She gritted her teeth and managed to stay confined, though she might not have lasted much longer if Jon hadn't released the button.

"How was that?" he now asked.

Darlene took a deep breath. "Ever been on a roller coaster?"

"Yes."

"Well, that last jolt was like being *under* the roller coaster." Darlene wanted to touch her pussy just to make sure everything was still intact and close to normal size, but of course her hands were still bound.

"Cool," Jon said.

Despite her strong will and determination, Darlene began to doubt that she could weather another jolt like the one that Jon had given her without breaking free—and going on a bit of a rampage. And she sure didn't want to do that. So maybe the time had come to say Uncle, or in this case, Editor. Maybe she'd just reached her limit, and she had to recognize that.

But before she could bring herself to give up, Jon said, "You answered my question so graphically, I'm going to answer yours. No, I didn't invent this particular goodie. Actually, the remote control vibrator has been around for a long time. But I figure two things. One, I thought we could have some fun with it. And two, I want to make a better model."

"Cool." Darlene echoed Jon.

He pressed the button and she braced herself for another shock. But this time, the surprise was...pleasant. The butterfly vibrated tantalizingly, caressing her pussy and playing with her clit. Darlene squirmed pleasurably, quickly wishing she could close her legs to hold the little critter more tightly. Of course she couldn't, and her restraints severely limited her desired movements.

Which was okay. With the steady buzz of the instrument, Darlene was coasting along at a steady pace of sheer sensation. Oh, yeah. She could have kept on with this all day.

The vibrations became more intense, which meant Jon must have increased the pressure on whatever button he was pressing. Darlene now fantasized it was his mouth on her where the butterfly was fluttering, that he was searing her with his kisses, bringing on the start of an orgasm.

Instead of his tongue, Darlene knew his eyes were on her. She looked over at him, wondering if watching her was turning him on—wanting him to be turned on by the sight of her thrashing in his bed. Jon had one hand on the remote and one hand on his huge erection, which now jutted forth from the fly of his black leather pants. Methodically, Jon was rubbing in time to her spasms. Darlene felt a twinge of regret. She wanted to be the one stroking his cock, but her hands were imprisoned. All she could do was watch him, which raised her excitement to nearly unbearable levels.

Her thighs twitched helplessly as the orgasm spiraled through her, fed by the butterfly and the sight of Jon masturbating, the tip of his cock now gleaming with pre-cum that she wanted to suck off him as an appetizer for the meal she'd make of him later.

Thought processes disintegrated as Jon ratcheted up the remote and shot her to a still higher level of feeling. Her orgasm gripped her from all sides, and—still bound—Darlene howled out her release in long, piercing volleys of sound. Jon's cum spurted forward, as he quietly gasped out his release. When Darlene began to subside, Jon gave the remote one more slam that rifled through her with an intensity that she was too wrung out to battle. She'd snapped off one leg chain and was about to break the second when Jon let go, and she was able to get her brain together. She did not want Jon to know she'd broken the link, and so she kept her leg where it had been—much easier when the chain had been intact.

Jon came over to the bed and sat down next to her, stroking her glistening pussy lips with his hand. He bent over and kissed her deeply. But Darlene couldn't give herself up totally to the kiss because of her disappointment that Jon had zipped his fly back up. Not that she could touch him yet.

"That was great for me," he said. "How was it for you?"

He was asking, so she'd answer. "Breathtaking, Jon. What do you have in mind to make it even better?"

He half grinned. "Just some random thoughts, so far. Nothing solid enough to talk about yet. And now, of course, I'm thinking about creating film that can record how gorgeous you look when you're playing with the butterfly."

"Lots to think about," Darlene said.

"Yeah," he laughed dryly. "But tonight's not about thinking. How about I release you from these cuffs? They won't work for what's coming next."

Darlene cringed, realizing he'd discover the broken chain—and who knew what that would set off. She wished now she'd learned how to fix things with the power of her mind. But she and Lynette had always blown off the Comte when he tried to teach them.

Jon was evidently going to arrive at the broken chain last. Of course, he moved so quickly, that didn't give Darlene much time to think of what she'd say. Sure enough, he was there.

"This one's broken." He held up both ends of the broken links in his hands and looked at her accusingly. "What happened, Darlene?"

* * * * *

Looking at the severed links of the chain, Jon felt a rush of emotion. On one level, he felt pissed that his sub disobeyed. As in deliciously pissed. Of course this gave him an opening to provide some much-needed lessons. Not that Jon needed an opening. Where none existed, he made his own.

But on a deeper level, Jon recognized he was in uncharted territory. He was on his own to figure his way with Darlene, a vampire. The thought of everything she was set his nerve endings on edge. He wanted to be with her, but it had to be on his terms. And, looking at the links, he recognized she was holding all the cards.

How could he get her to deal him in?

* * * * *

Darlene sat up so she and Jon were on the same level. Now she had to be honest with Jon. "That last time you shot the full remote power through the butterfly." She clamped her mouth shut.

He shook his head. "Tell me more."

Okay, here it came. "Those restraints were hard to take. As you know. I've mostly managed to submit to being cuffed, but that became a major struggle when you ratcheted the remote up to what I guess is full speed."

He nodded. "Yeah, I did pull the throttle all the way back a few times. Should have given you intense, mind-blowing pleasure."

She snorted. "Up in those registers, it was like I couldn't tell the difference between pleasure and pain. The pleasure was so intense, it became pain. You know?"

"Awesome."

"I suppose. But with the restraints, everything for me was magnified. And then when I came, and you put on that last burst, for just a second it was all too much for me to fight against any more. That's when the first cuff snapped. I was able to stop myself before I broke any more, but that took a lot of determination. I'm sorry, Jon."

"I believe you," he said, turning somehow sad. Darlene worried what that look in his eyes might mean for any future they could possibly have together.

He was sitting very close to her, his leather pants cool and smooth against her bare leg. Now he put his arms around her and pulled her to him for a kiss. Darlene's fangs had retracted after she came. They began to descend again, and she focused real hard on not piercing him. Jon probed her mouth, nibbling on her lips, running his tongue over her teeth—even the fangs. Darlene's clit vibrated in time with the rhythm of Jon's tongue on her canines. She'd always maintained there was a direct line from her fangs to her clit—now Jon was proving it. Darlene filed this fact away for use in a future Veronica book, then consciously refocused on the man at hand. The sight of him stroking himself flickered before Darlene's eyes, and she reached for the fly of his pants. This man had remained dressed way too long.

Jon grabbed her hand in a viselike grip and firmly pushed it off him. "I'll tell you when and how you can touch me," he hissed.

Darlene's first reaction—feeling very hurt by this apparent rejection—dissipated as she looked into his eyes. Jon was the one who was really hurt. Seeing the broken chain must have made him have to face how thin the veneer of his being the dominant with her was. If she wanted to be with this man, she had to agree to play by his rules. She knew that.

But a new thought began to work its way to her consciousness. If she wanted to be with him, the two of them needed to reach a whole new level of communication. Because willing as she was to submit to Jon, she also had her limits. And they had to come into the mix.

It wasn't like he was completely opposed to accepting Darlene's nature and its demands. After all, he'd easily agreed to her feeding from him. No way could he have had any illusions of being the dominant during that.

Or had he? Had he somehow framed the whole scene as him being dominant by allowing it to happen?

Before Darlene could follow this line of thought through to its conclusion, Jon took her by the hand and dragged her over to the chair opposite his bed. "You've been very bad, breaking the chain like that," he said icily. "I have to teach you a lesson. Now."

He handed her the discarded shoes and instructed her to put them on, which she did, quickly.

"Put your foot on the chair," he directed. Darlene was still wearing the butterfly harness, and the action of lifting her leg produced a swift, pleasurable friction.

"Now put your hands on your head, and leave them there. I want you to stay still." Darlene did as she was told.

Jon picked up a braided cat that he must have positioned on the table near the chair some time earlier. Darlene began to shiver in anticipation of what he was going to do next. Her pussy was so wet, she felt herself soaking the butterfly with her gleaming slickness.

Jon flicked the braided cat in the air, producing a sharp whooshing sound that stirred the air near her butt.

With the remote in one hand and the braided cat in the other, Jon positioned himself next to Darlene's rear end. Darlene felt the first jolt of the butterfly action. Grateful that she wasn't chained this time, she allowed herself to twitch satisfyingly.

"I told you to stay still," Jon hissed. He promptly smacked her bottom with the braided cat—nearly taking her breath away. Tears—more of shock than anything else—sprang to her eyes.

Then she scolded herself. Why should she be shocked that he'd use a braided cat on her—especially considering how they met? But darn, that bugger sure hurt. Talk about mixing pleasure with pain. As the butterfly continued to vibrate, Jon struck her butt with the braided cat—his rhythm almost as regular as the butterfly's.

Darlene longed to turn around and see if Jon was getting aroused by any of what he was doing to her. But he'd explicitly ordered her to keep her head and hands still. She was in enough trouble with him already after breaking her chains. She wasn't going to risk getting him any angrier with her.

With all the action going on, fore and aft, staying still was no easy trick. But Darlene wanted to prove to Jon how disciplined she was becoming. To her amazement, the braided cat's sting began to mix with the pleasure the remote produced in her, raising the intensity. Instead of cringing when the blows struck, Darlene found herself moving her tush to meet them, even when Jon upped their force and frequency.

Darlene was really getting into high gear now, her tolerance for both the braided cat and Jon's increased pressure on the remote growing as quickly as her pleasure mounted. Now that she didn't have to worry about keeping the restraints intact—despite Jon's continuing admonitions for her to stay still—Darlene was freer to get into the sensations bombarding her most sensitive places than she'd been before. Jon's whispers and grunts deepened and sped up in intensity with his toys, adding to the orgasmic mix beginning to explode around Darlene— deep in her core.

Now her fangs were fully descended, her pussy fairly throbbing with a climax that threatened to shoot her right through the ceiling of the penthouse. As she began to quiver with the irresistible force building in her, Darlene knew she could wait no longer to slake her thirst for Jon.

As the first wave of her orgasm spread out from her pussy, Darlene jumped up and whirled on Jon. As her eyes blinked, she caught sight of his enormous erection, and she wanted him in her. Thought was no longer possible. With a flick of her wrist, she tore the leather thong and butterfly off, flinging it aside.

She then grabbed Jon, threw him down on the floor, and sank her fangs into his neck as she inhaled his hot cock up into her throbbing pussy. As she drank, she arched her hips on him, raising her climax to almost unbearable intensity. If her mouth hadn't been otherwise occupied, she'd have been shrieking her release.

Jon moaned, and awareness returned. With a start, Darlene realized she'd sucked almost too much of his blood. From the look on Jon's face, in his eyes, he was perilously near the border of death—or transformation. Shuddering at how close she'd come to changing him—for she'd never have let him die—Darlene pulled her face back from his and struggled to calm her still pulsing fangs.

Though Jon had nearly passed out from blood loss, he was still rock-hard. Darlene rode his cock now, her hips pumping with all the hunger of what might have been the longest-anticipated orgasm in history. Her pussy gripped Jon's penis as she ground herself into him, sliding up and down, and, now that she wasn't feeding any more, howling sounds that probably reached the full moon shining down on them.

Just as she rode the last wave, Darlene felt Jon begin to come. He also looked as if he was starting to recover his senses, his usual color. He turned his head back and forth, shooting his cum into her with a series of grunts and the heavy panting of a man who'd run a race. When he stopped spasming, Darlene bent her head down to lick his puncture wounds—so deep it took several passes to get them to close completely. Wow, she must have been totally out of control when she plunged into him.

With his still half-erect cock deep inside her, Jon held her close. Darlene spread her legs out, deepening her pussy's hold on him. Both of them were slick with the fluids they'd given up. Darlene felt grateful to him for the orgasm—and for the closeness she felt with him now. Her ass still stung from the blows with the braided cat. She'd have to put some balm on it when she got home if she intended to sit at the computer any time soon and work on Veronica's story. But she didn't have to think about any of this right now. All she had to do was, as they say, be in the moment with Jon. Revel in the extraordinary adventures she'd been having with him—and, most especially, in her growing closeness with him. She wondered where their relationship was headed. All she knew was that she wanted more of everything with Jon—more of what they did together, more of what he knew about the scene, but most especially, more of him.

For the first time, she began to understand Lynette. A relationship did not have to have hearts and flowers, all the sentimentality Darlene had always cherished—the stuff she'd wanted to fill the Veronica stories with. Now Darlene knew there was a whole other way of looking at a relationship.

Was what she felt for Jon love? Darlene nearly sneered at herself. Who cared? Maybe she loved him, maybe she didn't. She could think about that another day. For now, the sex was hot, he got her heart beating and her fluids racing around her body. Did he love her? All she knew now was, he wanted to be with her, found her arousing. That was clear.

Which was why the next words Jon said had her shaking with disbelief.

Jon was stroking the side of her face with more tenderness than she'd ever known experienced with him. "I can't see you any more, Darlene," he whispered. His shaft went soft and fell out of her, leaving them both wet and cold.

Of course she hadn't misheard him. Her hearing was perfect — beyond perfect. She couldn't have misunderstood what he was saying, could she? Though she'd just told herself she didn't know if she loved him, Darlene's stomach lurched and her heart clenched into a tight hot claw at his words.

Darlene didn't want him to stop touching her face, but she had to raise her head to look at him. "What do you mean?" she asked, wondering if this was yet another of the games he played — the cruelest by far.

But he looked totally serious, his mouth a grim line that she longed to kiss.

"It's hard for me to talk in this position. Let's get up. Get dressed."

All Jon had to do was to zip up his fly and smooth his clothes, run a hand through his hair. Darlene dressed with vampire speed, which she'd thought would please him but seemed not to.

He led her over to sit on the couch, then sat opposite her. "Darlene, I've spent some of the most exciting hours of my life with you," he began.

This didn't sound like a typical farewell speech to her, so Darlene began to take hope. "So why..." she started to ask. He held up his hand in a gesture telling her to stop.

"I can't do this any more." He shook his head. "Darlene, the way you just attacked me, right after you broke the chain."

"I'm sorry." She hung her head. "I got carried away." She wanted to be close to him as she said the rest, so she got up and began to move to him.

He turned his head away and again repeated his stop gesture. "Please, have the decency to stay where you are. I can't say what I need to if we're touching."

"Sorry." Darlene subsided back into the loveseat. Her gut told her what he had to say was more negative than she could imagine.

"You got into it and got carried away, and there was nothing I could do to stop you."

Those damn fangs. Her bloody hunger. "I promise, as I get more used to you, to us, nothing like this will happen again. I started exercising control over myself, but I haven't got it all down yet. If you'd just give me another chance."

His eyes grew wide and he shook his head again. "Really. I need you to let me talk."

"Right," Darlene said, vowing to keep her mouth shut.

"I'm a fucking *dom*," Jon said. "I know you're new to the scene, but you must have a clue as to what that means."

"Dominant," Darlene said, before she could button her lip again. "And I'm a submissive."

"R...i...ght." He stretched the word out to three syllables. "And I'm the fucking King of Siam. You see, with you being a vampire, I fucking well know that I'm only dominant as long as you let me be. But you've got so much power, the moment you want, you can break chains. Hell, you could mop the floor with me, use my tired ass as a plunger for your toilet. I'm so outclassed by your power, I'm not even in the same ballpark."

His words stung. "I tried," Darlene said.

"Oh, yeah. You had to sit on your powers for you to go along with my plans. But no matter what you did, you couldn't refrain from breaking my chain. Hell, I'm probably lucky you didn't break them all. And then you attacked me, sucked my blood, and screwed me."

Darlene felt an actual blush rise and color her face. "I'm so sorry… I promise I'll do better in the future."

"That is so not what I want to hear from you," he said, shaking his head sorrowfully. "You see, it's not good enough for you to just pretend to go along with me. When you do that, you're the one in charge—which makes you the dom even when you play at being the sub. And that just doesn't work for me. Not at all." He looked away.

Darlene didn't know what to say. She knew that from his perspective, he was perfectly correct. Much fun as the sub's role was for her, she'd never be truly submissive to Jon—or to any mortal man. She couldn't be. That was her nature.

Jon acknowledged that he knew the same. "A vampire is the natural dom in any relationship with a human. I was stupid not to realize that as soon as you told me your true identity."

"No, Jon. You're amazingly intelligent. No one could ever say you were stupid."

"I can." He waved his hands in a gesture of futility. "I've been thinking. We have two options."

Darlene focused on the glimmer of hope he held out for her. Two options. She nodded, to show him she was paying attention.

"First is that we stop seeing each other," he began enumerating on his fingers.

She started to protest, but he held up his hand to stop her.

"I'm not saying that's what I'd prefer—just that that's one of the options. The second," he looked her deeply in the eyes now, "is that you do whatever the hell you have to do to make me a vampire." He looked over at her expectantly.

Darlene's shocked gasp escaped her before she could reflect. Jon didn't know what he was asking, what he was proposing to put himself through. Here she was the expert, and her jaw clamped shut with her rejection of his idea. "Absolutely not."

Though Jon raised an eyebrow, his face quickly resumed a mask of nonchalance. "Very well. You've made the choice. Go home now."

"Jon," she protested, "those can't be the only choices we have."

His face now relaxed into an appearance of reasonableness. "Well, I certainly can't turn you into a human. So unless you know something I don't, the two choices I've named seem to be our only ones."

"You have no idea what you're asking of me."

Jon sat back in his chair and crossed one leather-clad leg over the other. "That's right. I don't. I know only the most superficial things about vampire life—scarcely more than the average Joe knows. Tell me what I'm asking for."

"This is a big decision." Darlene longed to move, to pace up and down so she could disperse some of the energy roiling up through her, so she clutched on to her seat as an anchor. "First off, you know you'd have to die. Your life, such as you've known it 'til now, would be over."

Jon shrugged. "And I'd have immortality instead, right? That's what the common impression is."

"Well, yeah," Darlene said. "I mean vampires can expire, but most of us these days manage to survive for ages."

"Am I supposed to see a drawback in that?" Jon asked, his eyes gleaming. Darlene's heart fluttered as she imagined him as a vampire. Jon would be a powerful force to deal with, maybe even eventually on par with the Comte.

He frowned then. "Uh, if you did, what's the word?"

"Transform."

"If you did transform me, would that mean that we couldn't be able to play any sex games anymore?"

Darlene's lips twitched in an involuntary smile, wondering what thought process led Jon to such an idea. "Heavens, no. We don't operate under any such rules or laws."

"So that's not an obstacle," Jon said. "Unless it would make you dominant over me if you transformed me."

"It wouldn't. I don't think anything that exists in the universe would suffice to make me dominant over you."

Jon evidently liked that response. For the first time since she'd met him, he really grinned—lighting up his whole face. What a gorgeous man he was! Darlene couldn't help thinking what a shame it would be for him to lose his good looks to old age or the diseases that ravaged people.

"I like that." He uncrossed his legs and sat forward. "So, what's the hang-up? I want to be with you at a whole other level than we've been together so far. Darlene, what can I do to convince you?"

"Nothing." Now she did give in to her restlessness and stood. "Jon, I've never transformed anyone. It's just far too serious a step to take."

He looked up at her. "What exactly is involved?"

"You know. Basically I'd need to feed on you 'til you were close to death. And then you'd need to suck blood from me."

"Sounds pretty straightforward."

A small smile played on her lips. "It's not."

"Sit down again, Darlene."

She did.

"You say you've never transformed anyone else. But I don't really know what that means. How long have you been a vampire?"

She'd never told a human her death story before, didn't know how detailed and intimate she was going to end up getting now. Probably best just to begin by straightforwardly answering his simple question. "I became a vampire one night in 1972, while I was traveling in France with my best friend Lynette."

"You both became vampires at the same time?"

"Yes."

"Uh, did the same vampire transform both of you?"

"Oh, yes," Darlene said, her thoughts flicking to the Comte, his castle, and a stormy night with hundreds of candles casting a romantic glow.

He gazed at her as if expecting her to continue her story. Darlene shut up. After several moments heavy with silence, she said, "Look, maybe I should go."

Jon chuckled dryly. "I certainly can't keep you here. But Darlene, if you leave before we resolve this, I want you out of my life. Permanently and completely. I understand you can't be here with me if I don't give you an invitation or if I revoke the one I gave you."

"Something like that." His words fell on her like molten silver.

"So you really haven't been a vampire all that long, then?"

"No. Just over thirty human years. I'd be a middle-aged woman if I hadn't been transformed. Instead, I'm a young vampire."

"I like the sound of that. A young vampire. That's what I'd like to become. Tonight."

"Jon, I need to think about this, you know?"

"She's weakening," he said, his smile now broader than before. He stood up and went over to Darlene, holding out his hands to her. She grabbed on and stood up close to him. "I'm not too demanding. You don't have to decide to do it tonight. I want to come to your house tomorrow. That'll be soon enough," he whispered hoarsely.

Darlene grew aroused, but slapped that down. He was not going to get to her through more sex. She needed a clear head now. "It's really not that simple. A new vampire needs so much. A suitable coffin. Instruction in our ways... And what about this place?" she asked, indicating the condo.

"What? You think I'd have to give up my penthouse?"

"Don't you have heirs? People who'd step in to claim your worldly goods if you died? You wouldn't believe the mess Lynette and I had when we came back to San Francisco..."

Now Jon chortled. "No heirs. I've got the paperwork all arranged so that, even if I 'disappear', the condo and all my possessions are protected and still belong to me only. As to the coffin, are you telling me that you and your friend have only two coffins in your house? What do you do when you have guests? Send them to a motel?"

"Okay. So you've made arrangements and, yes, we do have extra coffins at our place." She paused. "I still won't do it."

Though Jon nodded curtly, the look in his eyes told her he didn't accept what she was saying. "Then tonight is goodbye."

"Why?"

"Because part of what I do as a dom is fuck with your mind. But I can't begin to do that when you've done the ultimate fuck of *my* mind."

"No, Jon. Even though I'm the vampire, you have well and thoroughly f…f…that word—with my mind."

"Trust me on this. *You've* done the ultimate mind-fuck here."

Darlene looked around the penthouse, this place where she'd been introduced to so much. "I need more time, Jon."

"I'll give you 'til tomorrow night."

Feeling like she was literally clutching at straws, Darlene said, "Right. Tomorrow night. My house at midnight."

Jon kissed her hard, running his tongue over her teeth, his hands rough on her breasts. "I can't wait."

Chapter Nine

From Veronica Vampira's Secret Diaries:
Many a dawn have I wept myself into ponderous, bleak slumber.
When, when will my true forever love approach at last to set me
free from the perilous bonds of a too, too sensitive nature? I
tremblingly quiver with anxious anticipation...

Even after her tears subsided, Lynette couldn't bring herself to work on their manuscript. She was just too miserable to create any fun and frolic for Veronica, despite her new wealth of experience in—and her quavery introduction to—love. Lonely as she felt right now, she was kind of glad that Darlene wasn't home yet. Lynette did not want Darlene to know how much Nick had gotten to her, how devastated she felt. Were those tears filling her eyes, tickling her throat yet again? She never cried, never had even before her transformation. But tonight she felt like she was turning into a waterfall. Maybe she was catching some sort of cold or something. Not. Old reflex. Vampires didn't catch colds.

They evidently didn't get the guy either.

Now the tears trickled down her cheeks. Lynette tried to focus all her powers on staunching the flow—to no avail. Within moments, she'd surrendered to a crying jag worthy of Darlene—or Veronica.

Just then Lynette heard the turn of a key in the front door. Shit, Darlene was home. Lynette swept her hand across her face, trying to banish the tears. Nothing much she could do about her wet, swollen eyes. Darlene walked into her office, took one look at Lynette, and began to sob loudly and wetly. That got Lynette started again.

The two friends ran into each other's arms and hugged. Then they went in search of tissues.

Darlene honked loudly into an extra-strength tissue, then asked, "What's wrong?"

Lynette crunched up her mouth and shook her head. Sniffling, she said, "You first."

"Okay. Come into the living room. Bring the tissues."

Darlene sat down on the couch, and Lynette pulled a chair over. The two of them looked so wretched, Lynette decided they'd better turn off the light. She considered lighting a candle, then realized it would bring back too many memories of how romantic her time with Nick had been. She was better off sitting in the dark. Besides, with vampiric eyesight, it wasn't like they couldn't see...

"Talk," Lynette said, choking on the word. "What happened tonight with Jon?"

"It was wonderful," Darlene said. She put down her tissue and wrung her hands à la Lady Macbeth. "So many exciting adventures we can give to Veronica. Our editor will flip." Lynette thought Darlene's face went kind of funny when she said the word *editor*, but she figured she'd ask her about that later. For now, Darlene's story was pouring forth with uncharacteristic speed and warmth. Darlene was tossing off all sorts of words she'd never used before—*scene, dom*—words Lynette wasn't quite sure she understood.

"That all sounds fabulous," Lynette said. "So how come the waterworks?"

Darlene honked into her tissue. Then she wailed, "He said he's going to break up with me—unless I transform him."

Lynette gasped. Talk about an ultimatum! "Did you explain to him exactly what he was asking?"

Darlene honked several times more and swallowed hard before she answered. "I *tried* to explain it all to him." She shook her head and threw up her hands, accidentally flinging a wad of soggy tissues across the floor.

Lynette scowled. "Tried means you failed, doesn't it?"

Darlene nodded sheepishly.

"Did you say you'd transform him?"

"Not exactly." Darlene sighed.

"What does that mean—not exactly? Did you tell him that you absolutely, positively wouldn't consider transforming him?"

"I guess not. He's coming here tomorrow night," Darlene said in a very little voice. "It'll be do or die. Literally."

"Here?" Lynette bellowed.

"I had to agree to something so he wouldn't just break it off with me and never see me again. Lynette, do you understand what that's like? I don't want to lose him. I can't face the thought of never seeing him again."

Boy, did she ever understand what that was like. Only she hadn't been lucky enough to get that kind of choice. But she didn't even have the luxury of wallowing in her own pain, not with Darlene about to take such a huge step with this Jon. "Do you think transforming him is the only way to keep him?"

Darlene nodded. "That's what the man said. And he's not one to waste words. You see, it's all tied up with his being a dom and my being a submissive. But once things start heating up for me, my being submissive goes out the window..." Her voice squeaked on the last word, and Darlene began to hiccup.

"I can see where submitting might become a problem." Lynette remembered how carried away she'd been by the time she finally let herself begin feeding from Nick, especially the first time. Nothing any mortal man could do would have stopped her. "But Darlene, there have to be other fish in the sea. He's only the first guy you've been out with in decades. You could look for some guy who's already a vamp. You wouldn't have to think about transforming him. Why are you going through all this agony over Jon?"

Darlene sprang up. "Lynette, I don't know how I can explain to you how special Jon is. I mean being with him is not at all the way I ever thought romance—or l-l-love— would be. You know, I expected it to be roses and candlelight, hearts and flowers, all that gooey stuff I've always adored. But with Jon, it's not like that. Nothing's soft or sweet—it's all leather and hard edges, pleasure that gets mixed up with pain. It's like hard rock instead of opera, you know?"

While Lynette wasn't sure she totally understood, she didn't want to interrupt Darlene's flow, so she nodded.

"Now I finally understand why you were always pulling me away from making Veronica as frilly and...sentimental as I wanted to. Jon's style is so much more...exciting." Darlene jumped up and paced back and forth several times. "I feel like I'm addicted to being with him."

Lynette groaned.

"So I just *couldn't* tell him a final 'no' tonight, you know?" Darlene flung herself back on the couch. "I just had to have some hope for tomorrow. All the tomorrows."

"What are you really saying, Darlene?"

Darlene looked her full in the face and began to tremble. "I think I'm in love with Jon. Nobody else could possibly fill my heart and all the empty places in me like he does."

Lynette felt miserable, but she couldn't give in to her own agony, not with her friend so distraught. Besides, Lynette was the strong one. She couldn't fall apart now, not when Darlene needed her. Lynette patted her friend's shoulder in solidarity and sympathy as her mind groped for what to do next. "So what are you going to do? Tomorrow night's going to be here soon."

"I don't know," Darlene wailed, giving herself over to a fresh round of tears.

"Say," Lynette said, blowing her nose again, "with all this crying, you must be building up a huge thirst. Want some blood?"

Darlene waved her hand dismissively. "I couldn't drink a thing," she moaned.

Lynette sighed. "Well, I'm getting thirsty. I'll go pour two glasses and bring them in. If you want to drink, you can. If not, well we've got enough that we won't miss any I pour down the drain."

* * * * *

While Lynette was gone, Darlene thought. Unfortunately, all her ideas just kept going round in circles, not getting her anywhere. Her friend returned with two crystal goblets of blood on a wooden tray. Darlene was impressed. Lynette would never normally go for the crystal, let alone bring everything in on a tray.

Lynette put the tray down and helped herself, taking small swallows. After several moments, Darlene also picked up a goblet and began sipping. "Hate for you to drink alone," she muttered.

When Lynette had drained her drink half down, she asked, "So he's coming here tomorrow night?"

"Right before midnight."

"Cute touch."

"I figured I didn't want to just roll out of the coffin and break up with him. At least this gives me part of the night to imagine that we still have a relationship."

"You *do* have it bad," Lynette said. Darlene caught a strange tone in Lynette's voice, like she was trying to convince herself that Darlene was farther gone than she was. Darlene began to suspect that Lynette was in deep waters herself, and she shivered. Usually her friend was the tough one.

"But what are you going to do when he comes?" Lynette asked.

"Who knows? Maybe I'll end up transforming him," Darlene said.

"That's pretty drastic for a guy you've just met."

"Yeah, well I'm feeling in need of drastic measures. Even though you and I both made sacred vows that we'd never transform anyone and contribute to the burgeoning vampire population, I might have to break my oath."

"The Comte will not be happy." Lynette shook her head. "Again."

Darlene shrugged. "I know. Maybe when he realizes how cool Jon is, and what he's done to make my life anything but dull and boring, the Comte might forgive me."

"Possible." Lynette didn't look convinced. "Although the Comte's more upset about our being nominated for that award than about overpopulation. So maybe he won't make a big deal..."

"But I just don't know. I think Jon's making his decision too quickly. I'd hate to be responsible for transforming him—and then have him find out he hates being a vampire. Oh, heck, Lynette, I love him too much to lose him. And I love him too much to cause him eternal regret. And now I've got less than twenty-four hours to make a decision. I probably won't sleep a wink." She thought for a moment. "But here I've been yakking my head off, not giving you a moment to get a word in edgewise."

* * * * *

"You used the L word," Lynette said, hoping to divert her friend from pursuing her story.

"So I did," Darlene said. "I can use it with you. It would probably freak Jon out. Maybe that's why I l-l-love him. But I've told you my story. What's happening with you and Nick? As cozy as you were when I left, I was kind of surprised that he wasn't still here when I returned."

Lynette's iron control of her emotions snapped, and, with Darlene looking on in horror, she burst into a fresh round of tears. Darlene patted her on the shoulder, making comforting little sounds. When Lynette continued to cry, Darlene took her into a full hug and just held her until her weeping subsided into soft sighs. Then Darlene stroked

Lynette's hair. Lynette lifted her head and asked for another tissue.

"What is it, Lynette? I've never seen you like this," Darlene asked, looking deeply worried.

Lynette tried to smile, which came out wobbly. She snorted. "I've turned into you, and into Veronica at her slobbering, sentimental worst."

Darlene looked like she was biting back a smile, despite her tears. "That's difficult to believe. Tell me why you think so."

Lynette bit her lip. Too hard. She had to staunch her bleeding before she could talk. "How can I explain? Being with Nick was everything all those romances we read and write always promise...and more. Hearts, flowers, gooey stuff. Heck, with him I felt like I was on the inside of a box of Valentine's chocolates."

"And you decided you don't want to be there anymore?"

Lynette laughed dryly. "*I* didn't decide that. *Nick* decided it for both of us."

"What?"

"I feel like all those too stupid to live heroines."

"Technically, you're no longer *living*," Darlene noted.

"That doesn't help," Lynette snapped. "Being undead is no excuse for being stupid. Here we have fantastic sex, so hot my toenails nearly melted, and next thing you know, I'm picturing the two of us in a cottage with an herb garden...with little heart cutouts on the front gate and a wreath of dried flowers on the front door. Smoke coming out of the chimney..."

Darlene's eyes grew wide. "Really? You were thinking all those things?"

"Don't rub it in," Lynette barked. She narrowed her eyes. "Don't you ever tell another soul what I'm confiding in you tonight."

"I wouldn't dream of it. Besides who'd believe...? But what happened?"

"*He* said it's getting too deep and intense too fast. That, get this, I'm *ruining him* for other women."

"Yuck. He's thinking about other women when he's with you?"

Lynette nodded solemnly. "Even though he claimed he's crazy about me. That he has all these feelings for me, and it scares the shit out of him. Especially after I invited him to share my coffin tonight. Just for making love."

"So he's scared. Did he get into the coffin with you?"

"Yeah. He was nervous at first, but then it was great." Lynette sobbed again at the memory of being with Nick in her coffin. The same place she was supposed to try to sleep at dawn.

"And they say we women change our minds. You fed from him, right?"

"Yeah. Darlene, I almost came just from how good he tasted!"

"Wow. Well, if that didn't weird him out of his head, I can't see why great sex or even a coffin would have that effect."

Lynette pursed her lips. "That's because we think logically. He thinks like a man. The long and the short of it is, he said 'Hasta la vista, baby' tonight. Permanently. He wants to forget me and our special bonds, and he wants me to forget him. And then he gave me a dildo and his very own personal copy of *Romeo and Juliet*. As if I ever could forget him." Lynette wrung her hands.

"As if you ever could," Darlene echoed a heartbeat later. "He shared his *Romeo and Juliet* with you? I never knew you even liked that play. You always made fun of me…"

A fresh torrent of tears poured down Lynette's face, and Darlene shut up.

The two sat in silence punctuated by the occasional sob.

"How could I have been so friggin' *stupid*?" Lynette asked rhetorically.

Darlene took her hand. "You weren't stupid. You were just being…well…a *girl*—one who put her heart out there and risked it all."

"Put my heart out there and got it stomped on," Lynette grumped.

"So you did." Darlene leaned toward Lynette, who met her halfway. The two friends sat with their heads together. Which still, unfortunately, did not provide them with any inspiration as to how to get out of their current situations.

As dawn was fast approaching, they couldn't sit where they were much longer. Feeling far more restless and unresolved than they usually did when they tottered off to their coffins, Lynette and Darlene wished each other a good day and prepared themselves for their rest.

* * * * *

Darlene, realizing with a pang how much better off she was than her friend, climbed into her coffin. But she felt so bad for Lynette that she couldn't gloat for even a moment. Knowing she had more control over her situation than Lynette had of hers—a complete reversal of their usual roles—helped give Darlene some more insight into Jon and his frustration. Being the dom was clearly a role someone who needed and wanted to be in total control would choose. Having that be impossible must be unbearably frustrating.

From this point of view, Jon had sacrificed a lot to be with her. Now, she felt he was proposing to sacrifice even more. More than he could possibly realize. Darlene and Lynette enjoyed being vampires, but she knew not everyone took to the transformation they way they had. Jon clearly had no idea that transformation to vampirehood came with no guarantees. From the outside looking in, he probably only saw the glamour of vampire life—none of the hard, or occasionally yucky, parts. It was her thoughts of the latter, along with the Comte's sanction, of course, that kept her from easily transforming Jon—or anyone.

So what should she do? Despite her earlier fear that she'd be unable to sleep a wink, Darlene quickly fell into a deep, dreamless slumber.

* * * * *

Lynette was so exhausted, she hoped sleep would come quickly. But her coffin still lay on the floor where she and Nick had left it after they made love. And, just as she'd been hoping when the night began, the coffin was filled with the scents of their lovemaking. The smell and feel of Nick, of their total intimacy within the coffin's confines, surrounded Lynette. Her skin tingled from the contact.

For a moment, she considered just switching coffins again, abandoning the one she loved. But it was too late for her to go through the house in search of another coffin to curl up in. But tomorrow and tomorrow and tomorrow…

All those tomorrows, centuries of them, without Nick. Lynette would have sworn she didn't have any more tears left, but now she found a whole new source. She had her cheek pressed to one of the Nick-stains on the purple silk when sleep at last overtook her.

* * * * *

Once he left Lynette's house, Nick should have felt relieved. But all he felt was empty. Maybe, he told himself, it was from all the blood she sucked from him. Or, more likely, from his giant climaxes.

He unlocked his door and turned on the lights in his cottage. Usually, coming home was enough to snap him out of any blues. But now he remembered Lynette's reactions to everything she saw. He glanced at the bare spot on his end table where he kept his *Romeo and Juliet.* Correction—where he used to keep it.

He sat down next to the table and ran his fingers over the spot, which now looked barren. So he'd get a fresh copy of the play. He was glad now that he'd given it to Lynette. After all, he'd treated her like shit.

Maybe he'd go to Verona. Some day. And not think about the vampire who loved *Romeo and Juliet.* And him. She loved him, in whatever way vampires could love.

He shivered. She so didn't fit in with his life plans.

Did she?

He staggered off to bed and did his best to sleep.

* * * * *

After Darlene left, Jon poured himself a Bloody Mary, light on the tomato juice. Then he sat down at his computer and started reading everything he could find about vampires on the Net.

Too bad most of the people who posted were people. Jon tried to find information from the source, but vampires appeared to be pretty closemouthed about their culture. At least on the Net.

He frowned. He'd been hoping to find some argument to convince Darlene to transform him. Or, maybe, something to convince him not to change.

He found neither, though he read 'til his eyelids began to shut at dawn. Though he hated to admit it, Darlene was damned important to him. Almost like love. Which he didn't totally buy into.

He wanted to be with her. Becoming a vampire was the only way that would work.

Now all he had to do was convince the woman with the teeth.

His eyes shut and, the computer still whirring, fell asleep on his desk.

Chapter Ten

From Veronica Vampira's Secret Diaries:
Love and wisdom…do the two ever make their arrival together?
Or am I desperately doomed to always be unwise, and therefore
subject to nasty, relentless, ongoing, disappointment in my
eternal frustrated quest for my prince, my one true love?

The next night, a fine mist whirled across the sky, thickening and coming down to land near the still rusty, decrepit remains of the old Dupont-Monroe Mansion. The mist slowly became solid, taking on the features of an elegantly dressed man, who looked around himself for a moment, curling his lips in disdain.

Laurence de Cormignac, the Comte du Montnoir, sighed and prepared to enter the house. In the time since his first visit, neither Lynette nor Darlene had contacted him with any information to show they were changing their lives in compliance with his dictates. Now he felt desperate, a sensation alien to him before his involvement with these two.

He glanced over to where his assistant for delicate matters, Monique de la Chauve-Souris, had just materialized. Pursing her brightly colored lips, she brushed off her black silk jumpsuit. "Are you sure it is absolutely necessary for me to remain here with these two losers?"

The Comte made a What-can-I-do? gesture. "Drastic situations call for drastic measures, chérie. You are the best, the top in the field for teaching even the most hardened cases to have some style."

She rolled her eyes. "Judging from the way this house looks, even I might be unbearably challenged here."

"Are you saying you cannot do this?" His voice broke on the last word.

"I'd never say that," Monique responded, looking almost bored as she surveyed the current state of her latest manicure. "After all, nothing is impossible for me."

He smiled. "Of course. You will come away with one more success on your résumé, and my reputation will be saved."

She looked at him full face. "And you will pay my price for this service."

"To the last Euro."

Monique straightened up. "Very well. Then we should not tarry any longer. Let us enter the abode." She stopped for a moment, listening. "But first, let us listen to the conversation they are having. Perhaps this will save precious time in fixing them."

"Very well," the Comte said, shaking his head. "Look at the two of them, still closeted in their home after all I said to them about getting out, livening up their…"

Monique yawned. "Don't be redundant, Laurence. Let me listen."

From the illuminated window that the Comte knew was the living room of the house, they distinctly heard the first speaker—Darlene—say, "We have to let Veronica try a little submission. You know, do a scene with Jackson whipping her."

"But that's so not Veronica. She's a romantic, not a submissive, for pity's sake."

"Are you saying a vampire maiden can't be both?"

"Well, yeah. There does seem to be some conflict between the two. And we don't want Veronica stepping so far out of character. Her fans will be disappointed if she goes from hearts and flowers to whips and chains."

"Whips and chains can be just as romantic as hearts and flowers."

"Neither is as romantic as a double-headed dildo!" Lynette's voice grew quite high as she pronounced this sentence.

The Comte began to smile—for the first time in three nights. "On second thought, perhaps I've underestimated dear Lynette and Darlene. Monique, it is possible your stellar services will not be required after all. Which would mean you could refund my deposit of ten thousand Euros."

Monique did not look happy. Then she bared her teeth in a smile that did not match the glower in her eyes. "My dear Laurence. I thought you were an intelligent man, but now I wonder." She paused for several beats before resuming. "Did you not read the fine print on the service contract you signed whilst engaging my services?"

"Of course. I read everything."

"Then you know that you should not even think about a refund. Or about canceling my services after you've dragged me to San Francisco. You will pay me my whole fee, or the fiasco of these two winning the Bicentennial Award for the Most Dull and Boring Vampires will be only a fraction of the misery that will dog you night after night."

He exhaled. "But of course." He chuckled. "I was just thinking out loud a bit, a harmless exercise in speculation. After all, the way they are talking now, the new vocabulary they have learned…perhaps they have indeed begun to have a life. If they will just provide me evidence to show the committee, we can both be on our way. If not, you will stay with them. I take nothing for granted, and I honor my commitments."

"No more idle speculation. And don't let a few words of conversation mislead you. After all, they might just have been looking at an Internet site or a catalog for the local store, Happy Humping. I myself have ordered from them."

"Those are possibilities," the Comte said, his face losing some of its previous glow. "Very well. Let's go in and assess the situation. Then we shall know how to proceed."

The Comte, being a gentleman of the old school, placed his hand on the small of Monique's delectable back to guide her to the front door. Monique promptly shrugged his hand off and hissed at him. He felt a stirring in his groin that was ill-timed. But damn, there was something about an uppity, independent woman…

* * * * *

Having decided that the manuscript their editor rejected was hopeless, Lynette and Darlene were hot and heavy into plotting out a new book. The doorbell's chime interrupted their discussion.

"Are you expecting anyone now?" Lynette asked her friend.

Darlene shook her head. "Jon isn't coming over 'til midnight. It's only ten. I know he's eager, but he's far too cool to arrive here so early. How about you?"

Lynette winced. After the way Nick had departed — less than twenty-four hours before — she knew better than to expect him. Still... Maybe he had changed his mind. Her heartbeat accelerated. And then decelerated. Whoever was at their door, she could sense it wasn't Nick.

"I'll go get it," Darlene said.

She returned a moment later with the Comte and some punk-haired vamp wearing black silk that looked like it was painted on and killer heels. "Look who's here," Darlene announced brightly. "Monsieur le Comte and his companion."

"Assistant for specialized matters," the woman barked. "Monique de la Chauve-Souris." Lynette held out her hand, but Monique made a disparaging sound and walked around the living room. She picked up a tarnished statue of Eros shooting an arrow, replaced it, and frowned fiercely.

Lynette looked at Darlene. What the hell? After years of benign neglect, the Comte was visiting their house for the second time in three days. And what the crying bat's blood was that...that...*floozy* doing at his side?

"We've both just come in from Paris," the Comte said. Uninvited again, Lynette mentally added.

"And we would appreciate some refreshment. I hope you have had a chance to purchase a greater selection..."

Lynette cringed, remembering that Darlene had been far too busy to shop.

"We've been out a lot since your previous visit. I'm afraid all we have to offer is still O positive."

Monique snorted. "And you thought they'd reformed," she said to the Comte. She turned to Darlene. "Very well. Please wash a glass and bring me some O."

Lynette couldn't believe Monique's bad manners. She also couldn't believe that, for the first time since she'd ever met her friend years ago, Darlene looked angry.

Despite how totally appropriate it would have been for her to boot Monique the hell out of their living room, Darlene bit her lip and went to the kitchen. Lynette winced as she heard Darlene running water. She sincerely hoped she wasn't actually washing a glass. Or that, if she did, she left lots of soap residue. Ingested soap could ruin a vampire's whole night.

Within moments, Darlene had returned to the living room with a tray bearing two goblets filled with O positive. She handed a glass to each of their unwelcome guests, who'd taken seats on the couch—Monique perched at the edge.

"You are probably wondering why I am here again so soon after my previous visit," the Comte said after a long swallow.

"Yeah, and why'd you bring Miss Congeniality with you?" Lynette blurted out. Darlene shook her head slightly, as if to warn Lynette from saying more.

The Comte put down his glass. The bat woman, who was taking minute sips, her lids hooding her eyes, watched him from over the rim of her glass. He cleared his throat. "If you will remember, when I was last here, I told you about the dreadful award you've been nominated for."

"The Bicentennial Award for Most Dull and Boring Vampires," Darlene rattled off in a dutiful voice.

The Comte shuddered. "Yes, *that* one. As I recall, I explained to both of you what a calamity it would be for all of us if you were indeed to receive this particular award. And that you were to take steps to remove yourselves clearly and distinctly from contention. Do you not recall this very conversation, my ladies?"

Lynette squirmed. She saw Darlene about to respond and got there first. "Yeah, we had that talk. Why is *she* here?"

"Madame de la Chauve-Souris is a well-respected, leading authority on taking the terminally dull and making them appear to have *élan*—style, chic."

"And you've brought her here to *our* house?" Lynette asked, her voice rising in outrage.

"And not a moment too soon," Monique de la Chauve-Souris sniffed.

Lynette hid her face in her hands.

"But we've both done many new and decidedly cool things since then," Darlene protested.

"What sorts of things?" the Comte demanded.

Darlene looked at Lynette, who'd dropped her hands. "You want to tell them or should I?" Darlene asked.

"Go for it," Lynette said, impressed with how much bolder her friend had become in a very short time.

"Well, we started off watching a threesome at Club Decadent, where a man asked me to dance. And then Lynette and I went to Happy Humping and we both met men, went home with them, and…"

The Comte leapt up. "But is this true, or is this more of your writer's imagination?"

"It can't be true," Monique chimed in from where she was sitting. "Happy Humping is a sophisticated shop, not some place for bumpkins."

Lynette let her middle finger express her opinion of Monique's opinion. After everything, she was not about to let this harpy come in and try to poison her feelings about the place where she and Nick first connected.

"That's nice," Monique snapped. "Grownup, sophisticated reaction. But what else could I expect from two cows like you?"

"Cows?" Lynette shrieked. She got up nose to nose with Monique. Actually more like nose to tonsils. Monique was rather tall.

"Out!" Lynette ordered Monique. "Get out of my house. Now. You are not welcome."

"As if I'd consider staying in a low-rent rattrap like this a moment longer." Monique humphed her way to the front door, then turned to address the Comte. "I will wait for you on this front porch. If you do not join me by the time two minutes have elapsed, I shall return to Paris alone. Either way, the full bill for my services will be on your desk first thing tomorrow night."

"But Monique," the Comte protested, following her to the door. "*Attendez*. Wait." She slammed the door in his face.

Lynette nearly smiled. She'd never before seen the Comte at such a loss. Maybe she should have agreed to take lessons from this Monique chick. After all, if she could reduce the Comte to such a state, she might have a trick or two worth finding out about. Guys probably didn't break up with her.

The Comte whirled on them. "You have told me nothing of these adventures. If what you say is true and can be verified, you will indeed be out of contention."

Now Lynette's temper really flared. "First, Monsieur le Comte, Darlene and I are never less than totally honest with you. Second, we have been too busy with our new adventures to contact you. Third, why didn't you just contact us for the information you wanted? It would have saved you a lot of bother—and we'd have been spared the displeasure of that creature's company."

"The time is growing short. In two nights, I must show the council proof that you are not appropriate candidates for the dastardly award—or your name goes on the, how do you call it? Ah, on the *short* list. Then, even if you don't win, your names will carry the whiff of taint."

Just then they heard a loud whirring from outside. Two minutes must have elapsed and Monique the Creep was en route to Paris. The Comte furrowed his brow. Then shrugging his shoulders, he said, "Let us sit. You must tell me of your adventures. And, *mes chères*, be explicit."

They were. The Comte asked many questions and took many notes. "This is a superb beginning. But have you no photographs, no proof of these stories that I can bring to the committee? Their saying is—*Talk is cheap*."

Lynette wondered whether the Comte was beginning to lose it. Maybe the mind started to go after the first five centuries—and he was an old one. Everyone knew vampires couldn't be photographed.

Darlene looked sad. "Jon wanted to take photos of me. But, even with all his high tech stuff, he didn't have anything that would work on me."

The Comte shook his head. "It must be a worse backwater here than I'd realized." He pulled something out of a pocket that looked like a slightly large leather box for carrying a pack of cigarettes. "Have you really not heard about this new invention, the Vampera?"

"The Vampera?" both Lynette and Darlene asked simultaneously.

"The Vampera. Everyone in Paris has one. Can take a hundred pictures from a single chip."

"That's incredible," Darlene said, her heart beating hard now as she imagined how Jon would react to this invention. Jon. She looked at the clock. He'd be here in a bit more than an hour.

The Comte shook his head nonchalantly. "Developed in the East. I understand the same group is now developing a video Vampera. Ladies, we can be in pictures. Welcome to the twenty-first century!"

"Does that mean that with one of these, we'd be able to be in photos with humans and other vampires?" Darlene asked.

"These Vamperas record every known creature on Earth—and probably some unknown ones as well," the Comte bragged. "So, is there any way of bringing these men you've found over here tonight—perhaps with some of their special gadgets and toys?"

The Comte's eyes took on a gleam that Lynette suspected was less patriarchal than he might have wanted them to believe.

Lynette felt her heart break all over again. Thank goodness, Darlene came to the rescue. "Jon, who's been my partner, is due to come here at midnight. As for Nick, well, he and Lynette have parted…" Trust Darlene to make things sound the best possible.

The Comte was thinking out loud again. "Of course it would be far better if I could photograph both of you involved with the men in these various activities. Still, it might just work with one man. After all, both of you could play these sex games with him for my Vampera. Yes," he said, stroking his chin, "this might very well be the solution."

The thought of becoming part of Darlene and Jon's scene gave Lynette the same sick feeling as drinking blood past its sell-by date. She snuck a glance at Darlene and quickly saw her friend felt the same.

Lynette began to protest. The Comte interrupted. "Distasteful as you might find this, is it not preferable to getting the dreaded Most Dull and Boring Vampires award?"

Lynette had to think hard about this. Talk about a rock and a hard place. And the hard place wasn't Nick's friendly erection…

Just as Lynette was going to protest to the Comte, the doorbell rang—again. Still not midnight, so it wasn't Jon yet. She hoped that Monique creature hadn't found an excuse for returning. "This place is turning into a regular Grand Central Station," she muttered. But secretly, she was more than glad to be saved by the bell—unless it turned out to be Monique.

Lynette flung the door open—and saw Nick standing there, his eyes filled with adoration.

"Nick!" she said, before flinging herself into his arms. He held her, whispering her name. And then she remembered that he'd removed himself from her life the night before. He was far too solid to be a hallucination. What?

"May I come in?" he asked.

She swallowed hard. "I'm glad you're here. For about a million reasons. But Nick, why *are* you here? Did you forget something, or…?"

"Can you ever forgive me for being such a stupid asshole?" he asked, his eyes now almost as filled with pain as hers had been.

"Nick," she said, stroking the back of his neck with her hand. "You're not a stupid asshole. Of course I can forgive you."

He sighed. "I can't be without you, Lynette. I need you in my life. I want you in my life. I love you. Now and for always, whatever that means."

Lynette grabbed on to each word he said and pressed it to her heart. He said he *loved* her—and he wasn't seconds from orgasm.

"Nick," she said, "oh, Nick." She couldn't think what else to say.

"Who is it?" Darlene called out, reminding Lynette that she and Nick weren't alone in the house.

"It's Nick," Lynette called out, her voice pealing like a bell. Nick had come back to her.

"Bring the man in," the Comte called out. Nick looked at her questioningly when he heard the Comte's deep voice.

"Who's that?" Nick asked.

"Long story. Come into the living room and I'll introduce you." Hoping she'd never have to let go, she took his hand in hers. Lynette had a moment's fear, thinking that if one vampire he loved — *loved!* — freaked him out, what would meeting the Comte do?

But it was too late to turn back. If Nick was serious about loving her, than he had to get comfortable with her family.

* * * * *

Nick, wanting nothing more than to get back to Lynette's coffin with her and show her the depth of his feelings, reluctantly followed her to the living room. He'd met Darlene at Happy Humping, and had of course seen her briefly the night before. He hadn't known the first time that she was a vampire, hadn't suspected how his life was going to change. And maybe end. That was what happened when...when a person became one of them. His thoughts were racing too far ahead. He'd made no actual commitments yet, but felt like he was sinking farther into this new reality each moment he was with Lynette.

Standing next to Darlene was an elegantly dressed man of about forty. To Nick he looked like the epitome of European charm and old money. Dressed impeccably, his black hair perfect. Was this Darlene's man? Nick remembered her being with a much hipper-looking guy at Happy Humping.

Lynette was gearing up to make introductions. "Monsieur le Comte, I would like to present Nick LaStrada," she said, looking at the other man. She turned to Nick. "Nick, this is Laurence de Cormignac, the Comte du Montnoir, just arrived from Paris."

Nick wasn't sure whether to bow or shake hands. The Comte solved that one by holding out his hand and, with an incredibly strong grip, nearly breaking Nick's. "Pleased to meet you..." Nick had no idea what to call the guy.

The other man released Nick's hand and gazed deeply at him. "You may call me Monsieur le Comte."

Nick tried to get his mouth around that one. Hadn't expected to have to trot out his rusty French tonight.

The Comte looked at Lynette. "This is the man you were telling me about?"

"Yes," Lynette said.

Little shivers began to run up and down Nick's spine. They'd been talking about him? Somehow that didn't make him feel real happy.

But the Comte looked quite pleased. "Then we can get some of those Vampera shots I need. We can get started..."

Just then the doorbell chimed again.

Vampera shots? What the hell did that mean? He didn't know what a Vampera was, but he didn't like the sound of it.

Darlene went to answer the door and came back with the guy Nick remembered from Happy Humping. She introduced him to everyone—Jon Torrance. Handshakes all around. Jon looked especially impressed to be meeting the Comte. Nick had a feeling this bizarre night was about to get a lot kinkier.

* * * * *

Jon had come to Darlene's house determined to live up to his ultimatum. As determined as he could be. If she wasn't going to transform him tonight, he was out of there. That's what he'd tell her. Much as he wanted to be with Darlene, if they couldn't do it on his terms, he had to quit. Now that he'd experienced being with a vampire, he wanted more. Oh, hell. He had to be able to convince her. Truth was, she'd caught his heart and mind like no one else ever had or ever would. He wanted to be with her, and the only way that could work was for him to turn vampire. Period.

But before he could launch into his argument, he met the Comte. His presence convinced Jon that something extraordinary was going on here tonight. Before he could ask Darlene for an explanation, the Comte, who looked quite pleased with himself, was explaining something in his heavily accented but excellent English.

"I am here on a very particular mission. It is important for the future happiness of both Lynette and Darlene that I return to Paris with proof of their exciting lives here in San Francisco. They have been telling me a bit about their adventures with you, and all the new things you have tried out with them."

Nick and Jon looked at each other questioningly. Who the hell was this Comte, and what was his role in the women's lives?

The Comte read their faces. "I am sorry. I have gotten ahead of myself. Perhaps we should all sit down, enjoy some refreshments. Darlene, Lynette, please bring appropriate drinks. Some wine for these gentlemen, and I shall have the usual." He led them over to the massive old dining room table and sat down at the head, indicating that they should all find seats.

Now Lynette and Darlene looked concerned. "Uh, Monsieur le Comte," Lynette said. "All we have is the O positive…"

His mouth curled in a moue of distaste. "Of course. Rome was not built in a day… Very well, we shall bypass the refreshments. Mr. Torrance, Mr. LaStrada, you are probably wondering why I am here with your ladies."

Both Jon and Nick promptly requested that the Comte call them by their first names.

"Ah, yes," he said. "The informality of this country always takes me by surprise. Very well, Jon…Nick." He paused. "I am here because I was the one who transformed both of the ladies. That is, the one who introduced them to their new lives." The Comte continued on with a summary of his very impressive autobiography and his current achievements and connections.

Jon's respect for the man kicked up a notch. He sensed the man's power. Jon's heart beat hard with the excitement of all the possibilities opening up before him through the sheer chance of meeting the Comte. He wanted to be part of the society he was just beginning to learn about. And he wanted it right away.

"I have come here tonight on a matter of some importance. As I was explaining to Nick before you arrived, I need to take photographs of the ladies involved in sexual activities with you two back to Paris. It is a matter of great delicacy."

Had Jon heard correctly? "But Monsieur le Comte, how can you possibly take photos of…the ladies?"

The Comte chuckled. "Of course, this was impossible until recently. But there is a wonderful new invention — the Vampera." Here the Comte, looking like he was filming the classiest commercial in the history of advertising, held up a small apparatus. "Using this, we can now photograph each other. Every type of creature has shown up in the prints. Admittedly the ghosts are not as detailed as one might hope…"

A Vampera. Jon was completely hooked. He needed to have one of those. He needed so much more than that.

He was sure the Comte would accommodate him. Hell, alien as the concept was for him, Jon was ready to get on his hands and knees and beg, if that's what it would take...

"So will the two of you assist me with this most important request? Do whatever it is you do with your ladies—allow me to take just a few quick photographs?"

No one said anything for a moment. Then Jon blurted out what was foremost in his head and heart. "I want to be a vampire. Right now. Tonight. I want to be everything you and the ladies are, Monsieur le Comte. And I want my very own Vampera."

The Comte's left eyebrow shot up. "Indeed."

Darlene looked less than pleased. "Monsieur le Comte, with all due respect, Jon and I began to discuss this yesterday. I have told him it's a big decision, to be made only after much thought. I also told him of the current ban on creating more vampires due to concerns about overpopulation..."

"Nonsense." The Comte snapped his fingers. "If I recall correctly, neither you nor Lynette spent much time thinking that night when you stayed at my château... As for vampiric overpopulation... What we are becoming concerned about is a lack of quality control as to whom we admit. But Jon Torrance is a fine candidate. Both of these men are."

Nick LaStrada looked a little green. He held up his hands. "I can't say I haven't given er...a *change* some thought. But I haven't decided yet."

Lynette looked as if Nick's statement surprised her. "There's no rush."

Darlene was frowning.

The Comte tutted away her concerns. "My dear, this is beyond wonderful. If we add a transformation to tonight's activities, we shall have the solution to the matter which concerns us here."

"I suppose you're right," Darlene said.

"Very well. The night is fleeting, and we have much to do. Let's start with the transformation, then the sex. Darlene, I would be honored if you would let me transform Mr. Torrance."

"Please," Darlene said.

"Very well. Let us set up. Who will take the photos?"

Jon would have been more than willing, but his role as transformee precluded that.

"I'm a techno-klutz," Lynette said.

"I'm worse than she is," Darlene added.

Nick, becoming greener by the moment, just stared at them all.

The Comte made a disparaging sound. "Oh, very well. I shall set up the tripod and put the Vampera on automatic." Within seconds, he had everything set.

He led Jon to a good Vampera angle. "All set?" he asked.

Jon was. But it all seemed so prosaic. Almost like going to the doctor for a tetanus shot. "Uh, shouldn't there be some more drama or something?"

The Comte looked a tad impatient. "Well, thunder and lightning are difficult to come by in San Francisco." He thought a moment. "Ladies, light some candles. Maybe put on a CD of violin music…"

Darlene and Lynette began to scramble.

"While they set up, I shall explain exactly what will happen. I am going to give you a puncture wound and suck your blood."

Jon nodded. "Darlene has done some of that."

The Comte nodded approval. "I am pleased to hear this. So you know, I shall put a slight hypnotic spell on you. The sucking process will feel most pleasurable, as it did when Darlene did it. Only this time, I shall suck far more than she ever has. I shall suck until I have nearly drained you. And then I shall pull away from you, give myself a cut on the wrist, and then you will suck your first blood from me." He sniffed delicately. "This part of the ritual always makes me sentimental."

"And that's it?" Jon asked.

The Comte, whose fangs were now gleaming brightly, nodded.

"But won't I need some training or something?"

The Comte indicated Lynette and Darlene. "I shall leave you in the most capable of hands. And I shall greatly look forward to hearing of your exploits. Because I can feel that you are destined for greatness."

"Let's do it."

Jon suppressed a faint shudder when the Comte first took him in his embrace and positioned his mouth for the bite. And then—though Jon hoped to stay conscious and aware through the whole process—everything went black.

* * * * *

Darlene felt like a coward, but she was so relieved that the responsibility of transforming Jon was out of her hands. And, somewhere deep inside, she felt thrilled that Jon was going to become a vampire tonight. Because she knew that they had to have a level playing field for them to really be in the scene they both wanted so much. Most of all, he really, really wanted to be with her. Maybe, in his own way, he loved her as she did him.

The three of them sat in a semicircle as the Comte fed off Jon and the Vampera clicked away. Darlene thought back to her own transformation. How strange that she'd never witnessed this very fundamental vampiric ritual before. When the Comte had transformed Lynette and her, he performed each ritual in a separate chamber of his château.

Now as she watched her lover lose the color in his cheeks, Darlene found herself melting in anticipation of how Jon would be after he fed off the Comte. With his enthusiasm, Jon would probably not need much of a recovery period...and then he'd be raring to go. Too bad his first real meal would be the O positive from her fridge... She'd never again let herself get into such a rut! Fortunately, Jon wouldn't have gotten jaded about blood yet...

* * * * *

Lynette held tight to Nick's hand, which felt as cold as hers. His eyes were riveted to the ritual. Lynette couldn't make out Nick's thoughts, and she didn't want to interrupt what was happening with ill-timed whispers.

With a grunt, the Comte pulled away from Jon's neck. He drew out a mother-of-pearl-handled pocket knife and traced a line across his left wrist, which he held up to Jon's mouth. Despite Jon's pallor and a look of weakness, he began to suck vigorously at the Comte's arm. In a surprisingly short time, the Comte pulled his arm away from Jon. "That's enough, my friend," he said, looking quite smug.

Jon licked his lips and flashed his brand new fangs at all of them in a huge smile. "At last," he said. He looked at Darlene with a distinctly lascivious expression. "Let's go, baby." He got up to walk toward her and stumbled, his fall broken by the Comte's outstretched arm.

"Though it won't take long, you do need a chance to come back to yourself. After all, you've just died," the older man warned affectionately. "Let us go sit down. Darlene, if you would fetch some refreshments from the kitchen, our young vampire needs his first meal."

Jon scowled. "Don't I get to feed off someone?"

"Time enough for all that later. Drink what Darlene brings you."

Jon complied, his face quickly regaining color. "Man, this is great." He looked over at Nick. "What do you say? Are you going to come over to the *dark* side?"

Lynette didn't enjoy Jon's mocking tone, or his challenge. "Nick hasn't given transformation any thought."

Nick rose, and for a moment Lynette feared he was going to take off again. "I'm ready, man. Beam me over or transform me."

Jon, who'd drained the pint already, got to his feet. "Best decision you'll ever make. Now that I'm here, I realize I haven't really changed. I'm still Jon Torrance— only better."

"Except you're dead and you suck blood," Lynette pointed out.

"Other than that. So, can I be the one who transforms Nick?" Jon asked, addressing his question to the Comte.

"We've been vampires for decades and never transformed anyone," Darlene said with a note of pride in her voice. "He's been a vamp for five minutes and wants to transform someone else already…"

Lynette took Nick in her arms. "Are you sure?"

He nodded. "I want to be with you, Lynette. You can't ever become human again, can you?"

"No," she said, feeling a rare pang of regret.

"Then this is the way to go. It didn't look so bad when the Comte transformed Jon. And then we can always be together."

Lynette nodded. She kissed him.

"A double-deader! Here tonight." The Comte was smiling broader than she'd ever seen before. "I do admire your energy, young Jon. But, although we don't have many rules in our initiation, new vampires would need to have their status for at least one year before they start transforming others." Then the Comte looked over at Nick. "If you will permit me, I shall do the honors. Let me just make sure the Vampera is set."

"He's AB negative," Lynette said, regretting that she wasn't going to get a last chance to sip Nick's delicious blood.

"First B negative, then AB negative. My cup surely runneth over."

When the Comte appeared satisfied with the Vampera, he took up his position and began to feed.

Lynette watched her lover go through the ritual that would make them equals. Nick's face looked almost as ecstatic now as when she'd been able to watch him during their lovemaking. This had to be a good thing.

Getting so much AB negative was such a treat, Lynette was afraid the Comte might forget himself and drain Nick. But she knew he was an expert. With a sigh, he drew away from Nick and repeated the earlier process of cutting his wrist. Nick sucked, then looked proudly at her—at all of them. He was even more devastatingly handsome as a vampire than he'd been as a man. Lynette wondered how long it would take to get a coffin built for two...

Lynette brought Nick his first pint, and he drank it down quickly. "Built up quite a thirst," he said.

The Comte chuckled to himself as he looked at the little screen on the Vampera. "These photos are marvelous." He brought them over to show the small group.

Jon started asking lots of technical questions. The Comte held up his hands. "Another time for all this." He looked at Jon with fatherly pride. "I shall return here more frequently... And you will visit me in France? Both of you. All of you. But first things first. I need some photos of your sex games to complete the portfolio. And then I shall leave here content to have accomplished my mission."

"Sex games?" Nick asked.

"Monsieur le Comte, with all due respect, aren't the transformation photos sufficient?" Lynette asked.

"They are wonderful," the Comte said. "But as neither you nor Darlene appear in either, they do not suffice."

"But after all that's happened tonight, we'd appreciate some privacy," Lynette said.

The Comte looked puzzled. "Modesty? About sex?"

Lynette didn't want to say the L word. Not before she had lots of time to say it to Nick. "How about if we just hold up some of our toys and smile for the Vampera? Like my double-headed dildo?"

The Comte considered. "I suppose that might suffice. After all, the Committee has known and honored me for many centuries…"

"I'm all ready to cuff and chain Darlene in a way she's not going to be able to break out of," Jon growled.

"Can't wait," Darlene said.

"Perfect. I shall take my shots, and then I must get my rest. A Transatlantic fight and two transformations in one night—not bad. And then back to Paris tomorrow night. Once the Committee sees my photos, we're saved."

Lynette and Darlene were about to show the Comte to the guest bedroom, complete with its velvet-lined mahogany coffin, when Nick stepped forward. "Just a minute," he said with new authority in his voice.

Lynette looked at him, startled. "What is it, Nick?"

"I and my new friend Jon here have just gone through a radical life cycle event."

"Yes, and?" Could Nick already regret his change? Though he hadn't been a vampire long, he was completely, one hundred percent, committed. As in no going back.

"Where I come from, life cycle events mean parties. You know, lots of food, music, good times."

The Comte looked on with admiration. "But of course. We must indeed celebrate tonight's momentous events." He gazed around himself and sniffed. "Obviously not here."

"I know the perfect place," Jon said. "Club Decadent."

Lynette and Darlene turned to each other. No surprise that Jon knew about Club Decadent already. "We know it well," Lynette said. "Sounds perfect."

* * * * *

Darlene couldn't believe they were returning to Club Decadent so soon after their first trip. But she also couldn't believe how much her life and Lynette's had changed since the first time. That night she didn't want to go. Both she and Lynette were like country mice in the big city. Well, maybe she more than Lynette. She'd felt lucky and special when Cornelius wanted to dance with her.

Now she'd be going there as part of a group with the elegant Comte—but, most of all, with her love, her man, her Jon. Veronica should only be so lucky.

After she and Lynette freshened up a bit, they piled into Nick's SUV. Lynette sat up front with him. The Comte sat in one seat, with Darlene and Jon in the back.

"Why can't we just fly there on our own power?" Jon asked.

"All in good time, old chap." The Comte chuckled. "Flight does require some instruction."

They chattered excitedly about everything Nick and Jon would soon learn all the way to the Club. Darlene couldn't help wondering if Jon was ahead of her in some vampiric areas already. Talk about a natural.

"The last show will be starting shortly," a snaky-looking maitre d' hissed as he showed them to a table set back from the action. The place was packed.

* * * * *

The Comte did not expect too much from this Club Decadent. After all, he'd seen many shows in France. But it was more than right for their party to come out to celebrate tonight's momentous events.

"What'll it be?" the server, another snaky type, slithered over and asked. Maybe tonight was snake night here.

Jon was about to order when the Comte said, "Permit me." His new protégé showed much promise. But after all, the Comte was in charge. He turned to the server. "AB positive cocktails for all." When the server left, he told his tablemates, "I prefer to start newcomers with positive, though it is less rare. Sets the right tone. Of course tonight is my treat."

Nick and Jon both protested, but the Comte insisted.

Their drinks arrived quickly. The Comte raised his goblet for a toast. "To long life, interesting companions, and abundant blood." The clinked glasses and drank.

Before he could ask the newcomers what they thought of the drink, an insistent drum beat and a spotlight in the center of the room announced the start of the show. A large snake with iridescent scales reflecting the light entered the circle, coiling and rising in hypnotic rhythm. Soon another snake joined the first. Guided by the drumbeat, the snakes rose to a great height and embraced, scale to scale, sliding over each other. Two more snakes joined the group, forming a tangle so that even he could not distinguish where one snake ended and the next began. And then another two joined the group.

As he watched, fascinated despite himself, the snakes formed a circle on the ground. Always undulating to the music, they began to vibrate, then tremble and grow. The scales became gleaming eyes and hair and nails, as the snakes transformed into their people forms, three women and two men.

Always moving to the music, still in their circle, they lay on their backs, alternating man, woman. Smaller snakes slithered out to the stage and began to entwine themselves around the legs of the people. The Comte felt a stirring in his cock as he watched one large snake start at the top of a woman's head and slowly slither his way down between her large creamy breasts. The woman rocked back and forth, her eyes closed and her face rapt as her companion circled her breasts.

The snake then wiggled down her belly to her pussy, where he buried his head. The woman arched her hips as the snake slid his long body through her pussy folds. By now other snakes were performing a similar journey on the people in the circle, and the Comte grew quite warm.

The smaller snakes moved to the center of the circle. The men, each extremely well-endowed, sported huge erections, as did the Comte. Like synchronized dancers, they got to their knees. Then each man lowered his face to the pussy of the woman near his head and his cock to the mouth of the woman below him.

The Comte could imagine Monique de la Chauve-Souris' lips around his cock, licking him, while he ate her delicious, high-priced cunt. His cock throbbed in anticipation of this delight as the snake people proceeded to give each other oral satisfaction.

Never breaking rhythm with the music, the performers writhed and arched, seeking their fulfillment. The music intensified along with the feeding frenzy. The Comte's sensitive eyes and ears gleaned the sights and sounds of multiple orgasms as the music hit a peak. And then, before his eyes, the people once again trembled and shook, and one by one returned to snake form.

All the snakes joined together in a large embrace, and then, to thunderous applause, left the stage.

The Comte was sure he'd be able to find this kind of performance, only of higher caliber, when he returned to France. He informed his companions of this fact.

* * * * *

Darlene had never liked snakes. Instead of looking at the show, she watched Jon, who appeared enthralled. When the performance ended, he drank some of his AB positive.

"Do you like it?" He grunted noncommittally. She hoped he could appreciate the gourmet drink. And then she realized that she'd spent the first few hours of Jon's vampirehood hovering over him. Jon's reactions as a vampire, even more so than as a man, were totally out of her control. Which meant she could relax. She hoped.

Music started, slow and sinuous just like the snakes' music. Nick took Lynette's hand and went out on the dance floor. Darlene closed her eyes and wished real hard for Jon to ask her. They'd never danced together, and she'd love to dance with him on this night of so many firsts. When she opened her eyes, Jon remained engrossed in his drink. He looked up for a moment and met her eyes.

"How about a dance?" he asked.

"Okay." She exhaled. Then she realized that the Comte would be alone at the table. When she started to say something, he waved his hand. "Go, children. Perhaps I shall find a partner and join in as well."

Jon led her out to the floor and took her in his arms. Thank goodness for slow dances. Darlene leaned onto Jon's firm chest. Always strong, now his arms felt incredibly powerful when he encircled her waist and pulled her to him.

So different from the last time here with poor little Cornelius trying to keep up with the music. Her body fit so perfectly with Jon's. He drew her even closer, and she could feel his erection press deep into her belly. She snuggled even closer.

"Thank you for everything," Jon murmured into her hair.

"Mmm," she said. "For what?"

"For my whole new life," he said.

"I can't take credit." The way he said it, he sounded like he was preparing to take off, leave her behind. He was free to go, which scared Darlene.

"I love you." He drew away for just a moment to gaze into her eyes and then he pulled her back.

Warmth flooded her. She never expected to hear these longed-for words from Jon. "And I love you," she whispered. He nibbled on the soft part of her neck, right below her ear. Soon, soon, their loving each other would include mutual feeding. Darlene's pussy grew moist.

The Comte danced by just then. Of course he'd found the most elegant woman in the place to be his partner. Dressed in gleaming scales, her tongue darted out to explore the Comte's face as they passed.

"Let's go home soon," Jon whispered.

Darlene pressed herself even harder against his erection and smiled.

* * * * *

By the end of the night out, the Comte felt very pleased with himself. He'd taken the number of his exquisite partner at the Club Decadent, a Madame Vivienne Vipère. Perhaps he'd phone her again when he returned to the city. Except for that fiasco with Monique de la Chauve-Souris, the night had gone far better than he'd have ever dreamed. And once he got back to Paris, he would deal with her. After all, who could ever resist him once he truly began to focus?

But he couldn't let himself be distracted. Before he could allow himself the luxury of a day's rest, he had more photos to take. As he planned to leave right after first nightfall, he needed to have everything arranged before he slid into the coffin.

First Lynette's room. He slipped in silently, catching Nick and Lynette in a hearts and flowers kiss, which he recorded on film. When they broke apart, he said, "Whenever you're ready."

Lynette and Nick together held up a huge dildo, two connected black penises with the heads facing away from each other. "Maybe just a shot where you show me how you use that," he said.

They both threw off their clothes. Lynette spread some cream in her slit and in the crack between Nick's cheeks. Then she wrapped both ends of the shaft in condoms, opened her legs, and wedged the dildo into her pussy. Nick got on his hand and knees and thrust his butt toward Lynette, who straddled him and positioned the free end of the dildo in his ass. The Comte couldn't help but see Nick's huge erection. Hmm, the Comte thought, sentimentally remembering his own first erection after his transformation. His cock began to harden now, and the

Comte regretted Monique's departure. He focused on taking his photos. Within moments, the Comte had several excellent shots—and, judging from their moans and movements, Lynette and Nick seemed to have totally forgotten his presence.

The Comte tiptoed out of Lynette's room and went down the hall to Darlene's. The enterprising Jon had already chained and manacled the totally nude Darlene to a bed. With his erection jutting out powerfully, he was tickling her with a feather—making her crazy. The formerly modest Darlene begged for a huge and powerful release. The Comte's erection grew along with his collection of photos. Darlene and Jon never noticed him.

With the sigh of a man who's completed a long night's work, the Comte climbed into his coffin, his own erection fully demanding his attention. He began to stroke his cock rhythmically, finding the pleasure sharper than he'd remembered. Now he'd satisfy this hunger with his own hand. Tonight he'd return to Paris...and Monique.

Epilogue
One year later

From Veronica Vampira's Secret Diaries:
Just got fitted for my black leather bustier. It rocks. So does
Vince, who's bringing the whips and chains tonight. Tomorrow
night, Luke and I are headed up the coast on his Harley. Hmm,
I've never done it on a moving bike before. Can't wait...

Soon after their transformations, Nick and Jon furnished their residences with coffins, which allowed the two couples to spend their days and nights in whatever locations suited their particular needs at the time.

Nick expanded his import-export business to include products for the vampire niche market. His human family appreciated Nick's new business successes and respected his desire to cut way down on travel. He and Lynette both became so busy, they had to schedule time to slow down together and smell the roses. Together they got into gardening by moonlight. They visited Happy Humping at least once a month to check out the new dildos and began to plan a trip to Verona.

Jon contributed his tech knowledge to the successful development of the video Vampera, which made him even more phenomenally wealthy. Jon continued to create and refine whips and different toys for the scene. He also began to develop chains and implements for the growing vampire bondage market niche and tried out all his new products and ideas with Darlene.

Lynette and Darlene got back into their writing groove. Much to their editor's delight, they had two bestselling Veronica Vampira novels that first year. Veronica became the heroine of a movie and a TV series. Her picture graced everything from lunch boxes to T-shirts. Lynette and Darlene could hardly keep up with the demand for Veronica stories. No more coupon clipping for them.

The Comte presented his pictures to the committee and succeeded in having Lynette and Darlene removed from consideration for the dreadful prize. He began collecting his papers for his memoirs. He continued to pursue his business affairs and Monique de la Chauve-Souris. But that's another story…

About the author:

Exploring the erotic side of romance keeps Mardi Ballou chained to her computer—and inspires some amazing research. Mardi's a Jersey girl, now living in Northern California with her hero husband—the love of her life—who's also her tech maven and first reader. Her days and nights are filled with books to read and write, chocolate, and the pursuit of romantic dreams. A Scorpio by birth and temperament, Mardi believes in living life with Passion, Intensity, and Lots of Laughs (this last from her moon in Sagittarius). Published in different genres under different names, Mardi is thrilled to be part of the Ellora's Cave Team Romantica.

Email: mardi@mardiballou.com

Website: http://www.mardiballou.com

Mardi welcomes mail from readers. You can write to her c/o Ellora's Cave Publishing at 1337 Commerce Drive, Suite 13, Stow OH 44224.

Why an electronic book?

We live in the Information Age—an exciting time in the history of human civilization in which technology rules supreme and continues to progress in leaps and bounds every minute of every hour of every day. For a multitude of reasons, more and more avid literary fans are opting to purchase e-books instead of paperbacks. The question to those not yet initiated to the world of electronic reading is simply: *why?*

1. *Price.* An electronic title at Ellora's Cave Publishing runs anywhere from 40-75% less than the cover price of the <u>exact same title</u> in paperback format. Why? Cold mathematics. It is less expensive to publish an e-book than it is to publish a paperback, so the savings are passed along to the consumer.

2. *Space.* Running out of room to house your paperback books? That is one worry you will never have with electronic novels. For a low one-time cost, you can purchase a handheld computer designed specifically for e-reading purposes. Many e-readers are larger than the average handheld, giving you plenty of screen room. Better yet, hundreds of titles can be stored within your new library—a single microchip. (Please note that Ellora's Cave does not endorse any specific brands. You can check our website at www.ellorascave.com for customer recommendations we make available to new consumers.)

3. *Mobility.* Because your new library now consists of only a microchip, your entire cache of books can be taken with you wherever you go.

4. *Personal preferences are accounted for.* Are the words you are currently reading too small? Too large? Too...**ANNOYING**? Paperback books cannot be modified according to personal preferences, but e-books can.

5. *Innovation.* The way you read a book is not the only advancement the Information Age has gifted the literary community with. There is also the factor of what you can read. Ellora's Cave Publishing will be introducing a new line of interactive titles that are available in e-book format only.

6. *Instant gratification.* Is it the middle of the night and all the bookstores are closed? Are you tired of waiting days—sometimes weeks—for online and offline bookstores to ship the novels you bought? Ellora's Cave Publishing sells instantaneous downloads 24 hours a day, 7 days a week, 365 days a year. Our e-book delivery system is 100% automated, meaning your order is filled as soon as you pay for it.

Those are a few of the top reasons why electronic novels are displacing paperbacks for many an avid reader. As always, Ellora's Cave Publishing welcomes your questions and comments. We invite you to email us at service@ellorascave.com or write to us directly at: 1337 Commerce Drive, Suite 13, Stow OH 44224.

Discover for yourself why readers can't get enough of the multiple award-winning publisher Ellora's Cave. Whether you prefer e-books or paperbacks, be sure to visit EC on the web at www.ellorascave.com for an erotic reading experience that will leave you breathless.

WWW.ELLORASCAVE.COM

Printed in the United States
29163LVS00003B/64-867